Archaeology **IN FICTION**

Archaeology **IN FICTION**

By Dr. Scott C. Viguié

Cover Illustration and Design by Matt Washburn

Interior Illustrations by Michael Mueller

Eureka Publications

Archaeology in Fiction

ISBN-13: 978-0615819785

Published by Eureka Publications

www.eurekapublications.com

To my wife Debbie, without whose love, support and encouragement this book would never have been possible.

Forward

This book is for fans of archaeology, both real and fictional. In these pages we will explore the top ten tropes of archaeology in fiction. We will discover why they are so popular, why they have persisted, and how they relate to the real practice of archaeology.

To aid in this exploration I have excerpted entries from the journal of archaeologist and adventurer, Charles "Tex" Ravencroft, whose exploits are further recounted in the upcoming novel, Tears of Poseidon, (Fall 2013). The illustrations provided throughout are those found in Tex's journals which he drew himself. As you can see, he had quite a sense of humor.

Author's Note

Not many professions have been as romanticized as that of the archaeologist. Whether you're a fan of Dr. Jackson, River Song, Professor Bernice Summerfield, Laura Croft, or the man himself Dr. Henry "Indiana" Jones, it is clear that action, adventure, mystery and discovery are not far behind.

Therefore, if you will forgive the indulgence, I feel obligated to start this discussion by saying Archaeology is the search for FACT …. Not Truth. If its truth you're interested in may I suggest you seek out a book on the philosophy of Doctor Who. So forget any ideas you had about lost cities, exotic travel, and digging up the world. We do not follow maps to buried treasure and X never ever marks the spot.

Well, all that is MOSTLY true. I am an archaeologist and while I learned more about septic systems than I would have anticipated, I did work on the island of Kauai, Hawaii which is very exotic and, yes, while in the field I occasionally wore a fedora like hat, and matching khaki shirt.

This is why I love this topic. The reality of archaeology has influenced its fictional counterpart and vice versa. So don your adventure gear, as we explore the realms of fiction in search of the facts of archaeology.

Dr. Scott C. Viguié

TABLE OF CONTENTS

RAIDERS OF .....

Dr. Henry "Indiana" Jones – Raiders of the Lost Ark

June 9, 1931

You never know what you're going to find until you find it. One of my professors used to say that. We all used to think he was crazy but he had been proven right more times than not. I stared at the little cat statue beneath the skull carved into the lava wall and thought maybe I was finally losing my mind.

I was standing on sacred ground, the royal coconut grove on the east side of the island of Kaua'i. I was searching for a goblet carved out of rock that had been used in times past for special types of rituals, those that involved human sacrifice. The legends about it were more unbelievable than that, but I didn't waste much time thinking about the other parts. The fact that it was rare and supposedly existed were enough for me. My search had brought me to this grotto. I had known we were on the right track when I saw the small pond. The cat and the skull were next to it, like some kind of diseased shrine.

1

The skull was leering, mocking me, and the cat was pointing as if he, too, were laughing. The cat was completely out of place, something that must have belonged to one of the foreign peoples who had been recruited to work the fields on the other parts of the island.

"You know, Tex, this would be a lovely site to put a hotel," I heard my traveling companion say. I ignored him. I just kept staring at that cat, the paw raised.

"I think he's pointing," I said.

"Pointing at a couple of fools. Time to give up."

"Never!" I told him. I had come too far to give up now. I stood, turned and dropped into the pond. I plunged beneath the waters, my hands feeling for anything that was out of place. My finger grazed something rough that was definitely out of place.

"Help me! There's something down here," I said.

Moments later we were hauling a giant clam shell out of the water. We tilted it so the water that had seeped into it could flow out. When we got it up on the shore we discovered that it opened fairly easily. Inside was something wrapped in ancient tapa cloth.

I unwrapped it and a small mug like object with hideous carvings on it appeared. I shivered slightly as my hand touched it, but struggled to ignore the feeling. I had found what I was looking for. There was something else wrapped in the cloth, though, a smaller piece of cloth. I unwrapped it slowly until I could see that inside it was a small gem, shaped like a tear drop.

It was dark hued, almost black with a purple glow to it. I blinked in shock.

"What is that?" my companion asked.

"Something that shouldn't exist," I said. I quickly wrapped the gem back up and shoved it inside my pocket. "We got what we came for, though," I said, standing up and hoisting the sacred goblet aloft. It was time to go home. I turned and took a step.

That was when all hell broke loose.

- Excerpted from the journals of Charles "Tex" Ravencroft

IN FICTION

Before either Indiana Jones or Lara Croft strutted onto the big screen, H. Rider Haggard wrote about the exploits of Allan Quatermain as he searched for fantastical treasures like King Solomon's Mines. Mankind has always been fascinated with treasure hunting and, more basely, treasure looting as evidenced by the looting done of ancient Egyptian tombs by the contemporaries of those who had died. This fascination has led to fantastic tales passed down through oral tradition and eventually books and then films.

Countless stories have speculated on what treasures the Pharaohs buried with them, what the Knights Templar might have hidden during the crusades, where pirates could have buried their treasure, and what valuables might have gone down with the Titanic. For each of these mysteries a dozen more exist as well.

A desire to uncover these mysteries and to find immense wealth has motivated many treasure hunters both real and fictional. Many of these fictional characters are aptly called tomb raiders as they have a specific treasure in mind and no real interest in studying a particular culture unless it can help them locate the treasure.

Many of these adventurers and treasure hunters call themselves archaeologists to lend an air of legitimacy to what they're doing. Some even hold seemingly respectable jobs. Indiana Jones is a professor at a respected university and works in conjunction with a museum. Daniel Jackson from the *Stargate* franchise works for the military exploring and trying to understand alien cultures. Other characters don't even pretend to be archaeologists, though. Benjamin Franklin Gates in the *National Treasure* films displays the same skill set as other fictional archaeologists, but he references himself as a treasure protector.

In fiction archaeologists often destroy, either on purpose or through accident or carelessness, important cultural sites or artifacts in the pursuit of whatever it is they are looking for. In the *Doctor Who* television series the character River Song routinely defaces ancient artifacts to communicate with the Doctor. Indiana Jones often destroys places of great cultural significance including the entire structure that housed the golden idol in the opening scenes of *Raiders of the Lost Ark*.

In fiction archaeologists are portrayed as the bold adventurers with a map in one hand and a gun in the other. They are action heroes who always get whatever they want and oftentimes save the world in the process. They are fearless, resourceful, oftentimes ruthless, and they know what it takes to get the job done.

IN OUR HEARTS

It is in the nature of man to crave a good story filled with adventure and discovery. This is why stories about adventurers like Indiana Jones and tomb raiders like Lara Croft remain popular. Mystery, adventure, and romance appeal to us on a very primal level.

As little children even simple games like Hide and Seek and Easter egg hunts foster this drive to ferret out what is hidden and be the one to discover the treasure before anyone else can. Kids dream of exciting lives filled with adventure and discovery. They want to be the policeman who figures out who the bad guy is and chases him down or the firefighter who rescues people from the burning building. Very few, though, actually grow up and take on jobs that have that much danger associated with them. The more structured and controlled our lives become the more we long for this kind of freedom and danger that is associated with the adventurer who dares to dream big and actually win.

In life there are so few chances to actually have clear victories or wins that the idea of a great quest with specifically stated goals is very appealing. Add to that the allure of a puzzle to solve, something that will test your intelligence, your dedication, and your skill and it's easy to see the appeal of these types of stories. Every year millions of people engage in puzzle solving which is why books of crossword and sudoku puzzles abound. That's because, unlike the rigors of life, these are puzzles that can be solved in a relatively short amount of time and actually give you a sense of completion. Life is rarely that neat and problems that finite.

It is also in human nature to want to acquire a landfall of riches. This is why people gamble, everything from slots to the lottery to bingo. The ultimate expression of that is the mythical treasure chest filled with gold and jewels that everyone in their hearts wishes they could find. This is made all the more tantalizing by stories of actual buried treasure and people who have discovered it. Even as we envy them their good fortune, some are inspired to go searching for themselves while the vast majority have to settle for watching other people live out their dreams and aspirations in fiction.

These human drives to discover great things and to solve puzzles drive fictional archaeologists and adventurers. They also drive real archaeologists as well.

IN FACT

In truth, archaeology started out as little more than grave robbing with many involved in the process truly being raiders. Archaeology began as a hobby for the rich and the curiosity seekers. Additionally, grave robbers participated in archaeology as a way to plunder the riches of a region and sell them on the black market.

Since then a great push has been made to make archaeology more of a science. The Archaeologist has transformed from the relic hunter who would search for a specific site which contains something of obvious economic value to the scientist who searches for answers about the past and the evolution of the human experience. The benefit of this transformation is that greater care is taken to preserve the areas being excavated and established procedures have allowed for greater conformity in the way digs are operated and artifacts catalogued. It also has provided legitimacy to archaeologists and allowed them to negotiate with world governments to gain access to sites safely and legally for the good of all concerned.

In one of those facts can be stranger than fiction moments, it was actually Thomas Jefferson, the third president of the United States, who is credited with being the father of modern archaeology. He excavated an Indian burial mound taking meticulous measurements and recording everything he found. Also, instead of starting from the top and digging down, he cut a chunk out of the side so that he could observe the stratification, setting the standard for years to come.

Thanks to his efforts and those of many, many others, today's archaeologists are scientists who carefully study, observe and record the past trying to understand and draw meaning from it while trying to preserve it as best they can. While there can be moments of significant scientific breakthrough, the vast majority of the work is tedious and time-consuming and you can work for days or even months without finding anything of intrinsic or cultural value. So, given that archaeology is not what fiction led us to believe it was, why devote lifetimes to studying it?

Man has always been curious about the past. Since the beginning humans have told stories about their origins and shown an interest for the things that are older than them. Amateur archaeologists, mostly taking the form of antiquities collectors, have existed for millennia. Within the last several decades a change has come about. Greater emphasis has been placed on careful study of archaeological sites and artifacts rather than grave robbing. Advancements in technology have served archaeology well in the last few centuries. The question remains, though, who does archaeology serve?

While it can be said that archaeology serves the truth, perhaps the real answer is that archaeology serves mankind. Archaeology is studied by various peoples and groups for different purposes. Historians are interested in uncovering cultural context for the major events of our past. Governments throughout history have used archaeology to solidify their own power and promote nationalism. Scientists seek to shed light on the ancient past with an eye also to the future. Individuals look to archaeology to sate their curiosity. A study of archaeology can therefore be said to illuminate the past, serve the present and give hope for the future.

Archaeology seeks to uncover the truth of human experience. In the four corners of the earth, in radically different climates and thriving in different types of cultures that experience has been basically the same both generally and often specifically. Man's needs have not changed much since the beginning. Humans are still in need of warmth, food, and companionship. Therefore, the majority of human existence both in the past and in the present is spent in pursuit of those things. This fact provides a basic framework for studying past cultures whether they be bands of hunter-gatherers or mighty civilizations that conquered half the known world. Even as these broad areas of human existence are constant, there are striking similarities in the specifics of lives lived so long ago with those lived now. There are even remarkable similarities between disparate cultures separated by time and space.

Some things haven't changed much through the course of human evolution. Some modern problems have roots that go far back in human history. Deforestation and air pollution have been problems for thousands of years.[1] Traces of opium in a Cyprus vase from 1500 B.C. are evidence of drug use and a

---

[1] Colin Renfrew and Paul Bahn, Archaeology: Theories, Methods and Practice 4th Ed. (New York: Thames & Hudson, 2004) 243.

possible drug trade in the eastern Mediterranean at that time.[2] Also, people have been trying to severely alter their bodies since some of the early humans, including Neanderthals, practiced skull shaping by binding the heads of infants or otherwise putting pressure on them.[3]

Some positive things remain constant throughout history as well. People have been using cookbooks to make their meals since at least 3,750 years ago, as evidenced by 3 Babylonian clay tablets which contained 35 recipes for different meat stews, a dish which is a favorite even today.[4] Mustard, olive oil and butter have been identified on potsherds including those from Neolithic lake dwellings.[5] A 12,000 year old human burial containing the remains of a puppy show that dog has always seemed to be man's best friend.[6] Along with the dog, horses have also long been faithful companions and servants as evidenced by a picture of a horse wearing a bridle from the end of the Ice Age.[7]

Perhaps even more amazing are the similarities not between past and present but between ancient cultures. In Alaska volcano warmed caves preserved bodies. The living would occasionally wipe down the bodies or heat them over a fire to dry them. Some had hearts removed and dry grass placed in the cavity.[8] Although most of the work of preserving the bodies

---

[2] Ibid., p. 284.
[3] Ibid., p. 451.
[4] Ibid., p. 288.
[5] Ibid., p. 283.
[6] Ibid., p. 300.
[7] Ibid., p. 300.
[8] Ibid., p. 68.

was done by the environment, the care that was taken with them, especially the removing of organs is reminiscent of Egyptian culture which also used organ removal as part of mummification.

Both the Incas and the Egyptians exhibited great engineering skill by moving massive stones. Noone has yet been able to figure out for certain just how they were able to accomplish these amazing tasks.[9] Additionally, pyramids appear in South America, Asia, and Africa. What about this structure appealed to these ancient peoples of very different cultures and geographic locations? Is it pure coincidence or did it serve some practical or psychological purpose? Maybe archaeologists will one day know the answer to this or perhaps it will always remain one of the mysteries of human existence.

Even as archaeologists discover more about the past, they are helping modern man. Illuminating the past also sheds light on the present. Archaeological finds can be used by many different people for many purposes. Apart from satisfying man's perpetual curiosity, a study of archaeology can serve the present in several ways, including: agricultural, constructional and medicinal.[10]

The study of archaeology is starting to produce benefits to agriculture. Modern scientists are spending a lot of time and money to find new, better ways to grow food and other crops with limited resources. While these scientists work on new techniques, others are looking to very old ones.[11]

---

[9] Ibid., p. 322.
[10] Ibid., p. 558.

Archaeologists and other scientists have made great advances in studying a variety of past farming techniques. They have also reproduced them in an effort to discover even more about the ways ancient societies farmed and lived off the land. Understanding of this area can also help illuminate other areas of archaeological inquiry. Scientists have even formed an Iron Age experimental farm showing greater crop yields than expected which could mean larger populations than previously thought and very strong houses.[12] Aside from illuminating other areas of study, archaeology can also help with modern agricultural needs.

The Incas built stone canals to bring water down from streams to irrigate their fields. After the fall of the Incas, the canals fell into disrepair. Modern scientists and workers forming the Cusichaca Trust have cleared and restored two of these canals. The results are astonishing in that now 150 acres of previously unusable land are now flourishing around the town of Patallacta.[13] The stone canals are just one example of how the past is benefiting the present. Scientists are learning that ancient peoples who occupied areas with harsh climates or barren ground had worked out solutions to these problems that will also work in the present to help benefit many third world countries.

As scientists continue to study the archaeological record, they may find more evidence of

---

[11] Ibid., p. 557.
[12] Ibid., p. 281.
[13] Ibid., p. 558.

the ingenious ways in which our ancestors learned to work even the most inhospitable lands. This can only benefit future generations of farmers who struggle to keep up with demands to feed a growing earth population. Scientists are also discovering that many of the difficulties we face today were also known to our ancestors. Recent study has shown that mankind has had problems with destroying his environment long before modern cars and factories led to air pollution. Deforestation and other land misuse were common even before the time of Christ.[14] Air and water pollution were problems as well.[15] Perhaps further study in the areas of land conservation, environmental issues and archaeology might benefit each other.

Archaeology also serves the present in the area of construction. Architects have taken the past and made it a part of modern day architecture aesthetically in beautiful, often dramatic ways, but there is also a great deal to be learned about the construction of ancient buildings and monuments. There are many mysteries, though, that still escape the archaeologist and the architect. The Anasazi erected buildings in New Mexico in the 10th century A.D. whose height wasn't rivaled until skyscrapers.[16] No one has yet fully answered the question of how the Incas and the Egyptians both moved massive stones in their construction projects. When these and other questions are answered, it could revolutionize the construction

---

[14] Ibid., p. 243.
[15] Ibid., p. 263.
[16] Ibid., p. 271.

industry or at least the way people think about the engineering feats of ancient civilizations and how they tackle the challenges of the present.

The desire to advance medical knowledge is another reason to study the past. While many people think that medicine only became a legitimate field of practice in the last few centuries, even mankind's ancient ancestors were concerned about their health and well-being. In the Americas, amazing, ancient surgical tools have recently been discovered.[17] The earliest evidence of dentistry comes from 8,000 years ago.[18] The question researchers are now beginning to ask is, what can these and other discoveries tell us about our ancestors in a way that helps modern medicine?

Archaeology has begun to help scientists shed light on some modern medical problems. In Australia, the examination of ear-canal pathologies in ancient Aboriginal skeletons may help pinpoint causes of chronic middle-ear infections experienced by a high number of modern Aborigine children.[19] Just as archaeology can help make advances in medicine and other sciences, the advancements in these fields serve to shed light on the past. Researchers have recently used DNA to show relationships within groups and ancestors. A study of the DNA of modern Jewish rabbis showed a common linkage around 650 B.C.[20] which would seem to substantiate claims that the

---

[17] Ibid., p. 458.
[18] Ibid., p. 455.
[19] Ibid., p. 558.
[20] Ibid., p. 229.

rabbis are descended from one man, perhaps even the brother of Moses as told in scriptures.

All of these discoveries and advancements have the potential to change our world view and even the quality of life for future generations. While archaeologists may not discover an actual fountain of youth, their work can still aid other scientists in improving and perhaps even extending modern life. While at first blush it's not quite as glamorous sounding, the truly amazing part is that unlike the fictional archaeologist, the real archaeologist has the capacity to make discoveries that will benefit all mankind.

THE SEARCH FOR FACT NOT TRUTH

Dr. Henry "Indiana" Jones – Indiana Jones and the Last Crusade

July 14, 1931

Met with Nathaniel Grant today at his office at the Smithsonian. He took the sacrificial goblet off my hands just as we had arranged. He seemed very happy to have it.

I told him about some discrepancies I noticed in some of the displays under his care. He didn't seem as concerned as I would have liked. We had an interesting conversation about the nature of truth. I feel like there's something he's hiding from me. I, of course, am hiding things from him.

He asked me what was next and I told him I didn't know. He said he could throw some work my way if I needed it. I didn't want to tell him yet about the gem, not until I've had a chance to talk to Dr. Reid about it. I'm afraid I know what Dr. Reid is going to say already, but I need to gather all the information I

17

can, figure out the facts before I start speculating about what it all means. I have a meeting set up with him in three days.

- Excerpted from the journals of Charles "Tex" Ravencroft

IN FICTION

Fictional archaeologists are always seemingly running all over the world looking for the truth. Almost inevitably, whatever myths or legends associated with their quest turn out to be the truth. Thus they are constantly seeking out the big mysteries of history, famous lost artifacts and cities, and the true origins of some items and structures.

When Indiana finds the holy grail, Daniel learns that aliens did indeed construct the pyramids, and Milo discovers Atlantis, all these things are exactly as fantastical as the audience expects. Seemingly all explanations can be found in the supernatural or in technology so advanced it either comes from an alien culture or appears to.

Even though Indiana tells his archaeology students that if they want truth they should take a philosophy class, he is just as guilty of buying almost instantly into all the mythology as all the others and following the legend instead of the facts. Of course, because it's fiction, that turns out to be the right answer. Whatever clues or facts a fictional archaeologist uncovers, they ultimately lead right to a greater truth. Nor is there anything that can't be explained or understood even if that explanation requires an act of God. In the real world, archaeologists have to spend much more time with facts than chasing after truth.

IN OUR HEARTS

As human beings, we are obsessed with the truth. We are obsessed with both exposing the truth and concealing it. In courtrooms you swear to tell the truth. Superman stands for truth, justice, and the American way. The *X Files* reminded us that the truth was out there. We keep the truth of painful things from others to spare them. As kids we play truth or dare hoping for either really juicy dirt on each other or the opportunity to put each other through insanely torturous tests. (Both of which were not until recently designed to turn us into the ideal reality show contestants.)

The problem is that the truth isn't always as black and white as we would like it to be. It can be subjective, and it can often rely greatly on our point of view. That can be a disheartening thought. Even in a world that's growing increasingly muddled and where things aren't always so clear cut we still desire absolutes.

Sometimes we put this in different terms. We want clear victories, obvious paths, closure on painful events, and road signs along the way to tell us what we need to know. It is because life can get so messy that we cling more fiercely to the idea of good and evil, lie and truth. The archaeologist, as Dr. Jones pointed out, does not search for "truth" since it is so subjective. He instead searches for "fact" which is not.

IN FACT

The difficulty with treating archaeology as a science lays with the reality that it actually takes a great deal of intuition and guesswork, especially given the scarcity of the data for many cultures, to come to conclusions about artifacts and other found items. There is a lot of science used including geology, chemistry, and biology in the study of archaeology. However, these sciences all deal with factual things. The archaeologist must often intuit the use of an item or the significance of its placement.

Some things are fairly straightforward, vases can be used for a number of purposes and we find them today intact and filled with things not dissimilar from what modern day jars and vases hold. Other things, however, are more difficult to categorize, especially given the tens of thousands of years of cultural evolution separating the user and the discoverer. For example, archaeologists 50,000 years from now might believe that remains of television sets were primitive altars, and that homes with multiple ones represented either homes of priests, or the extremely devout.

Archaeology, like all sciences, seeks to prove the validity of the theories of the archaeologist. This is the heart of the scientific method which revolves around creating a theory, testing the theory and drawing conclusions based upon the test results. Archaeologists do not lack for theories, there are many theories regarding most aspects of the discipline and most ancient peoples. In fact it often seems that there are far more theories than there are actual facts to either refute or prove those theories.

Some people treat their theories like fact before analyzing the results of their tests and occasionally even before doing any testing whatsoever. This is not only bad science; it is bad stewardship of public trust and funds and only hurts the discipline. Only those things which have been tested and analyzed and proven true can be labeled as "facts". Even this, though, is a difficult determination because, unlike some of the other sciences, some things in archaeology are not readily explained by a closer look with a microscope or the latest DNA analysis. The reality is that with even the most sophisticated tools, some elements of archaeology require the use of educated guesses which often are little more than the opinions of the people putting them forth.

This is problematic because every human has opinions, the ability to reason in this way and to communicate those opinions clearly are one of the things that separate man from animal. Individual backgrounds including experiences, upbringing and even racial or religious factors make up a person's world view and color their opinions. Thus, even the most conscientious archaeologist is still drawing conclusions about the significance of a piece of pottery

21

or a cave drawing based on his own world view and not the view held by the people who used the pottery or created the cave drawing. With this built in difficulty, it falls upon the individual archaeologist to do everything he can to carefully record and analyze, trying to distance himself from his own world view, a task which is never easy. It also falls upon other scientists and students to carefully analyze those results with an eye to understanding that they are not infallible but at best only a likely explanation for a past event, object, or belief. However, with awareness there is hope for the future.

Still, it is vitally important that archaeologists base their theories on the facts without trying to make their facts fit their theories. This seems like it should be the logical course of action, but it's amazing how many times the facts get ignored in the search to "prove" some political or cultural "truth". One of the most dangerous aspects of archaeology is that there are many individuals and institutions who shun the facts in favor of a certain story they want to tell, a particular reality they want to believe even if it's not in keeping with the facts at hand.

Fights have broken out, careers have been ruined and professional relationships destroyed when archaeologists decide to favor preserving the accepted story and their own beliefs about an idea over facts and evidence. The debate over Clovis versus Pre-Clovis is just one such issue which has divided archaeologists.

For years it was believed that the Clovis Indians were the first people in the Americas. When information came to light suggesting that there were people in the Americas before the Clovis sites, many archaeologists stuck their fingers in their ears and refused to listen. Their reasons were many and varied, but it all came down to a desire to preserve the existing story that Clovis came first. Entire careers and a whole field of study had been based on this premise and facts that suggested otherwise were seen as personal attacks and were responded to with venom. Instead of embracing the new findings as exciting and an opportunity to expand our knowledge of the early civilization of the Americas, many archaeologists tried to suppress, or at the very least, ignore the new information. Many archaeologists have found it nearly impossible to gain funding to continue this new research.[21]

Unfortunately this is not the only example. The discipline has been hurt time and again by archaeologists who seek to promote their own work and interests over the pursuit of facts. It could take centuries to undo all the harm that has already been done both deliberately and accidentally.

Research methods have evolved and researchers have grown aware of many cultural biases that have colored or limited their results. Previously even gender biases have impacted the interpretation of archaeological data. Part of the problem results from the fact that hypotheses aren't created in a vacuum. They are based on the researcher's own life experiences.

---

[21] *Can You Dig It? Archaeologist works to overturn long-held theory of when people first came to the Americas,* http://www.utexas.edu/features/2005/archeology/index.html, (accessed July 23, 2006).

Even interpretation of data can be suspect because we can only interpret the data in terms of our own physical and spiritual frameworks and understanding. We can never fully understand the meanings attributed to different artifacts by the people who created and used them, but we can hope to understand the similarities to our own tools, art, and ceremonies and thus find connection. This can lead to differences in archaeological interpretation and different individuals holding passionately to their view of archaeological "truth". When these passions hold sway it can cause archaeologists to turn on each other, hurting each other's careers and reputations, either intentionally or unintentionally and even causing physical harm such as a fist fight that once broke out at a world conference.[22]

If the truth can be unconsciously skewed or distorted by the beliefs and opinions of the unwary archaeologist, then the truth can be completely twisted by those with a vested interest in making sure a particular viewpoint is followed or another one is squashed. Part of searching for the truth is admitting when it takes you in unexpected directions and disproves commonly held beliefs. The archaeological community at large has had some problems with this. The truth is not always appreciated or acknowledged when it goes against accepted concepts. In fact, some archaeologists have even had their careers ruined for telling the truth.

---

[22] Colin Renfrew and Paul Bahn, Archaeology: Theories, Methods and Practice 4th Ed. (New York: Thames & Hudson, 2004) pp.50-51.

As disturbing as this is, individual archaeologists are not the only ones who can have agendas which affect research and can skew the truth of a find. Governments have strong motivations to use archaeology to connect them to the past or help foster a sense of national and cultural identity. It's a way of legitimizing the present and elevating their nation above others.[23]

Most modern nations attempt to use archaeology to reinforce certain ideas. While he was in power Saddam Hussein had a mural constructed which depicted him as Nebuchadnezzar, thus tying him to a great king of the ancient empire that occupied the same land as modern day Iraq.[24] Sometimes, peoples have even used their claims to the past to hinder modern archaeological efforts. This is especially true of some Native Americans who have demanded the return of all ancient bones to be buried, claiming all ancient skeletons as their ancestors, regardless of the evidence.

Of especial interest is the case of the Kennewick Man found in Washington State. The skeleton appears to be that of a 19th century white settler, but was radiocarbon dated to 9300 years ago. Scientists were eagerly trying to study this specimen but were hampered in their efforts by demands for his return to native peoples for reburial.[25] Such cases have necessitated court action. Arguments are springing up about who owns the relics of the past. Do they belong

---

[23] Ibid., p. 548.
[24] Ibid., p. 548.
[25] Ibid., p. 555.

to the people who currently occupy the land or are they a symbol of man's shared past and so the property of all humans?

It is possible that in the near future national and international laws governing archaeology will have to be reexamined to more fully and equitably answer these questions. What is clear is that such actions by different governments and peoples hinder the pursuit of facts while they seek to preserve their own particular story.

The desire to preserve the story has had disastrous results for both individuals and whole nations. When truth is sacrificed to make way for pet theories or to justify genocide everyone loses. It is amazing that some archaeologists have allowed themselves to be used to promote certain stories at the cost of the truth. While they are working to preserve these existing stories, there is much research and discovery that is not being done or is being blatantly ignored. This is just one of the reasons why it is essential that archaeologists study the facts at hand, carefully piecing together a picture of ancient cultures that is plausible, but open for change if new evidence comes to light.

Unlike the movies in real life and real archaeology there are very few neatly wrapped up endings or conclusive proof for particular theories in any timely fashion. Real archaeology requires a lot of patience, persistence, and the ability to not let the story drive the action but the foresight to have the discoveries help shape the story. Archaeologists who adhere to the standards imposed by scientists are careful to examine all their facts for what they can reveal instead of twisting or suppressing those that don't fit their ideas and theories.

70% of All Archaeology is Done in the Library

Dr. Henry "Indiana" Jones – Indiana Jones and the Last Crusade

July 17, 1931

Met with Dr. Reid in the library. That's where the man spends every free second of his day. I've always been of the opinion that he has more knowledge crammed into his head than a library twice that size could hold. I told him so and he just chuckled. His cat was with him, just like it always is.

I showed him the tear-shaped gem and he stopped laughing. He seemed very hesitant to touch it. When I was in school Dr. Reid would always lecture his classes about not jumping to conclusions, about taking all myths with a large grain of salt. He would become very worked up about it and rant against what he called para-archaeology. Deep down, though, I always suspected that he was a believer.

He demanded to know where I had found the gem and I told him. He said he believed it was made of orichalcum, the mythical metal used in Atlantis. He said he believed that the gem was one of the rumored "Tears of Man", three gems that could help reveal the location of the sunken city. At first I thought he was joking with me, but I quickly realized he wasn't. I had read descriptions of orichalcum before and my first thought upon seeing the gem was that had to be what it was. I was hoping I was wrong. I've never been a big believer in most mythology, particularly Atlantis. I know, though, that the gem is unlike anything I've ever encountered. I also know that when it is held in the palm of the hand for any period of time it superheats, far beyond the temperature of the skin on which it is resting. I have nearly burned myself twice with it. It's purple-black shimmer also begins to turn to red.

I asked Dr. Reid if he had any theories about where the other two "Tears of Man" might be. He said he had a few, but that if he was right they would not be easy to obtain...

- Excerpted from the journals of Charles "Tex" Ravencroft

IN FICTION

Fictional archaeologists often do a small amount of research, finding one or two key texts or historical footnotes to set them off on their quest. Sometimes these first clues aren't even written, but some bit of oral history passed on to them or even a bit of intelligence provided by a colleague or even a stranger. This nugget of information is enough to set them off on a glorious quest to retrieve whatever it is.

In *Raiders of the Lost Ark* men are sent from the government to question Indiana about what he knows regarding the Ark of the Covenant. He gives them the typical Sunday School answer and admits to not knowing much more than that about it. When he tries to find the real expert on the subject it turns out the man is dead but he has left a crucial artifact with his daughter Marion. A rival archaeologist is already digging in Egypt, but we don't see him doing the work to ascertain the exact location to be digging. Everything happens in a whirlwind of action with one clue leading to the next and then on to the Ark itself. It is possible that Belloq or the Nazis he was working for spent years researching before they started digging for the Well of Souls, but it seems unlikely in the context and flow of the film.

In the *Stargate SG-1* series Dr. Daniel Jackson is frequently shown doing research, but the time he spends researching pales in comparison with the time he spends in the field. The same is true for the vast majority of fictional archaeologists.

IN OUR HEARTS

For most people research sounds unpleasant. It's a reminder of days spent in school, homework and papers that kept us from playing and hanging out with our friends, and tedious hours reading boring things just because some capricious teacher told us to. This is why many people prefer their puzzle solving to be more active, more action-driven instead of more information driven. The truth is many more people would probably enjoy and embrace the idea of researching a topic if it was something of interest to them or something that they could see an obvious benefit from.

Of course, in films and television they assume, and rightly so, that the audience will only sit there and watch someone else read for so long without growing bored. Watching someone else read denies the spectator a chance for discovery or joining in on the excitement. It's more interesting when the camera actually shows us the critical piece of paper that someone is looking at so we can read along. However, that only works on short passages of text. Almost by necessity then does the fictional archaeologist skip the vast majority of the research phase of his mission. Real archaeologists can't afford to do that.

IN FACT

When an archaeologist is preparing for an excavation, they first do all the research they can. They head straight for the library and look up everything they can on existing archaeological reports for the area which could include maps, field notes, illustrations, lab test results, and diagrams of any objects that have been found. This helps them better understand what they're looking for, what they might find, and be prepared for anything unexpected.

When no such previous archaeological reports exist they then turn to other sources to gather information. They might look to geological reports, surveyor's maps, and historical accounts about the site. A thorough researcher will even take into account local legends and myths which might give him a better idea of what to expect.

There are two basic types of archaeology: text aided and non-text aided. Text aided archaeology is the study of events that have happened within the historical record. These are events that have occurred during the time of written language or those that predate it but have been similarly recorded. This type of archaeology relies on both physical evidence and written records. This study can be used in conjunction with examination of existing sites, or can even be used to help pinpoint the location of new sites. In this way a Viking settlement in Newfoundland was discovered because of clues in medieval texts.[26] In a similar way, Troy was discovered by a direct reading of the primary source material. Written texts can add a layer of richness and understanding when used in conjunction with physical finds. Non-text aided archaeology is the study of events that predate the historical record. This type of archaeology relies on physical evidence only.

Modern archaeologists who practice text aided archaeology are still trying to sort the myth from the

---

[26] Colin Renfrew and Paul Bahn, <u>Archaeology: Theories, Methods and Practice 4<u>th</u> Ed.</u> (New York: Thames & Hudson, 2004), p. 77.

history in historical documents. The farther we get from the physical and temporal origin of these documents, the more difficult this becomes. The Bible, a document much younger than many studied by archaeologists, has been consistently read and followed since its formation and yet modern Bible historians and theologians debate about the meaning of key passages. Matthew 5:29 exhorts believers that they should pluck out their eye if it causes them to sin. While most would agree that this is a metaphor, an occasional zealot has argued that it should be taken literally. Scholars also debate heatedly about what the affliction is that the apostle Paul complains of over and over again in his letters. Some say it is a physical malady, such as near-sightedness, while others claim it is a spiritual fault. If the Bible, which has been read and followed since it was written can cause so much confusion, how much more difficult is it to interpret documents belonging to cultures that have been dead hundreds or even thousands of years for which we have no frame of reference or modern understanding or even oral tradition?

Thus the job of the text aided archaeologist is not an easy one. It is difficult to sort fact from fiction and even to identify locations and events by the records we have of them which are often incomplete or make references to things we don't understand.

The development of a written language in a civilization helps to record events, communicate information, and capture ideas. Most ancient civilizations developed their own writing systems which were used by their own people and even occasionally shared with other civilizations with which they did trade. These written documents are often a great aid to archaeologists as they try to understand more about the culture and daily life of people who lived thousands of years ago. Many ancient writings have been translated, but some languages, such as the writings of the Harappan and the Indus, have yet to be deciphered.[27] Modern writing systems are descendants of these ancient ones. The ancient Phoenicians used an alphabetic script that was a predecessor to the modern alphabet.[28]

Ancient writings are a great aid in piecing together the history and culture of our ancestors. They also present some unique challenges, though. Chief among these are problems with translation and interpretation which we will discuss in depth in a later chapter.

On top of these problems with translation and interpretation of ancient texts, two other difficulties face archaeologists. Sometimes the written record is sketchy at best. Even when records can be found intact the archaeologist then must ferret out the facts from the fiction.

Sometimes ancient texts have been lost in whole or in part and what we know of them comes from references by other writers. This makes it difficult to fully study a culture when only fragmentary or secondary records exist. In this way we know that the Greek writer Hellanicus had a writing entitled

---

[27] Christopher Scarre and Brian M. Fagan, <u>Ancient Civilizations 2nd ed.</u> (Upper Saddle River, New Jersey: Prentice Hill, 2003) p. 18, 162
[28] Ibid., p. 221

"Atlantis" which was written before Plato's account. Unfortunately only fragments still exist and it does not offer much help to the archaeologist researching Atlantis.

The other problem with written records is that archaeologists have to decide what is fact and what is fiction. While mythology is important, it can sometimes be difficult to distinguish from history. These determinations are often left to the discretion of the archaeologist who might choose to correctly or incorrectly label something as history rather than myth. There is also the risk that the written record has been falsified in some way to serve the agenda of the people writing it. This practice was often widespread in Egypt where it was common for pharaohs to remove traces of their predecessors from history.

Given the importance of research when studying new sites or trying to draw conclusions about old ones, it is vital that archaeologists publish their findings. After the archaeologist has posited a theory, gathered evidence, and analyzed it, he must draw his conclusions and make them known. In this way not only can his work be analyzed by others, but also the knowledge he gained can be disseminated throughout the community where others can learn from it and build upon it. Perhaps one of the greatest tragedies in the field is the tiny percentage of archaeologists who actually publish their findings. For example, only 13 percent of the digs carried out in Israel in the 1980s have produced reports.[29] It is astounding how much

---

[29] Colin Renfrew and Paul Bahn, <u>Archaeology: Theories, Methods and Practice 4th Ed.</u> (New York: Thames & Hudson, 2004) p. 573.

work is being lost because the primary archaeologist either refuses to publish or leaves only scattered, unintelligible notes and dies without sharing what he learned. The results from the findings of the Dead Sea Scrolls went unpublished for years,[30] depriving other scientists of an opportunity to study them and the world from knowing their contents. Archaeological treasures like these should not be jealously horded by a few scientists, but shared with all for the greater understanding of all.

Archaeologists spend a lot of time in the field and in laboratories but by far they spend the most time doing research and taking and transcribing notes and reports of their own. It's how we preserve the information we have gathered to aid those who come after in their continuing study.

---

[30] Ibid., p. 573.

We Cannot Afford to Take Mythology at Face Value

Dr. Henry "Indiana" Jones – Indiana Jones and the Last Crusade

September 1, 1931

It was all true, I realized with a sense of shock. I stared around me, torch held high. My Indian guide had abandoned me a quarter mile from the cave entrance, telling me the place was considered haunted, cursed by his people and that none would approach it.

"I have already taken you too far," he told me.

I understand the power of myths to affect people that powerfully and so I didn't try to argue with him. He had promised to wait no more than four hours for me and since the way back wasn't easy, I knew I had little time to accomplish my task. I had continued on alone finding the cave entrance with a little difficulty.

I had come inside, not sure what I would find, never expecting that it would be just as the reports had said. Dr. Reid had shown me a copy of the Phoenix

Gazette article from April 5, 1909. He'd said I would be unwise to dismiss the claims of what had been found in a cave in the Grand Canyon, as unwise as those who had in the past denounced the existence of Troy. He was also convinced for some reason that one of the "Tears of Man" could be found here.

I couldn't help but wonder why the Smithsonian hadn't already thoroughly investigated and catalogued this place. I'd have to remember to ask Nathaniel about it later. At the moment, though, I was grateful that it appeared untouched so that I could hopefully find what I had come for.

I was looking at a full Egyptian burial in one room of what appeared to be a massive cave system. It looked old and authentic. The sarcophagus loomed in front of me as I tried to find a place to set my torch... [here he details more of what he found in the chamber]

...I was staring at a golden death mask. Just below the right eye was a single tear. I leaned closer, my heart beginning to race. I saw a hint of purple. I touched it and could feel it growing warm then hot. I removed my hand and saw it now glowing red. It was the second tear. Dr. Reid had been right. I pried it up and carefully wrapped it in a bit of cloth and concealed it in an inner pocket.

I didn't know how much time had passed, but I needed to leave before my guide abandoned me. As I hurried from the caves, I realized I could no longer afford to ignore mythology as I had.

- Excerpted from the journals of Charles "Tex" Ravencroft

IN FICTION

Fiction is resplendent with examples of archaeologists and adventurers setting off on fantastic adventurous in search of the objects and locations told of in myth. In most of these stories the myth always turns out to be real. Indiana Jones is responsible for tracking down the Holy Grail from Arthurian and Christian mythology. Allan Quatermain discovered *King Solomon's Mines*. The popular *Stargate* television shows made great use of Egyptian, Arthurian, and Atlantean mythologies.

In fiction myths are almost always proven true. Even if there is some debunking that happens there is just enough room left for doubt so that the viewer or reader can draw their own conclusions and choose to believe that the myth was real.

The hero may start as either a believer or disbeliever in the myth he's chasing after, but by the end when the myth is proven true he is a believer. In *Indiana Jones and the Last Crusade* we have an example of both. Indy doesn't appear to give too much stock to Holy Grail legends whereas his father has devoted his life to studying them.

The hero serves as a reflection of us, either in an initial state of belief or unbelief, and the journey he goes on is one that quenches our own thirst for adventure, romance, and knowledge. That's one of the reasons why we love these types of stories.

IN OUR HEARTS

Everyone loves a good story and that's precisely what mythology is. Myths are good stories told to enlighten, educate, entertain or illustrate. Myths often offer larger than life characters and fantastic solutions that we would love to believe are actually true because they are so much more exciting and emotionally satisfying than everyday life.

Take the Ark of the Covenant for example. We are told in the scriptures that the wrath of God would kill any man who touched the Ark. While many take this at face value and consider that it involved a direct act of God, others have looked for a mechanism that might have been set in place to accomplish it automatically. Several people of various levels of credibility have put forth theories in the past decades that the Ark was actually a capacitor of some kind and that touching it would result in fatal electrocution. If it were true this would mean the instructions God gave on how to build it created something that would function from that point forth without supernatural intervention. It makes a certain sense that appeals to the skeptical. Regardless of what the truth may be with regards to The Ark, storytellers will usually use the more fanciful version when utilizing a myth.

Imagine watching the part of *Raiders of the Lost Ark* where the Nazis open the Ark and Indy tells Marian to close her eyes. In the film we see the Angel of Death swirling around and turning from a beautiful figure to a hideous one that kills everyone who has laid eyes on it. It's an intense, amazing scene. Now imagine if the men lifting the lid off and those next to them were simply electrocuted and fell down dead. It's far less dramatic and leaves the problem of all the other Nazis present who didn't touch the thing being still alive. Also, if it just turned out to be a capacitor and not something more supernatural, the government would have no need to lock it away inside that warehouse at the end. Regardless of what a person's beliefs on the nature of the Ark are, most people would be forced to admit that the direct intervention, supernatural answer makes for a much better story!

Nine times out of ten the myths make for better stories than the facts surrounding events and objects that inspired them. We can see this principle at work even in our own lives. Think of some of the events from your childhood or even your college years that have since taken on a life of their own in your stories and become far more epic than they originally were. By the time your kids or grandkids hear those stories, they have begun to take on the quality of myth and it's hard to separate the fact from the embellishment. If the story is good enough, it will live on after you and when your grandkids pass the story down to their grandkids it will bear very little resemblance, if any, to the actual event. History will become legend and legend will become myth.

IN FACT

It is one of the jobs of the archaeologist to find the facts at the heart of every fiction. By their very nature the veracity of myths is instantly suspect. Not only is there the danger that each generation has embellished the story but there is also the danger that real details have been lost. Have you ever tried telling the same story to a bunch of your friends and seeing who can remember all the details and what gets changed? If ten people who know you can't keep a simple story straight, imagine what tens of thousands of people trying to pass a story through two millennia or more will mess up.

That's why mythology can't be inherently trusted and taken at face value. There is also a danger that if a researcher is too heavily influenced by the mythology of a people, a place, or an event that it will skew his own findings and that instead of reporting the facts and trying to assemble theories based on those facts, that he will instead be slanting the facts to fit the theory he is holding. The careful archaeologist observes and records first and theorizes later based on the evidence he has collected. Otherwise it would be the historical equivalent of a detective walking into a mystery and declaring "the butler did it" before he even knew if there was a butler within a three-hundred mile radius who had any connection to the victim.

On the other hand, even though mythology is inherently untrustworthy, it does not mean that it should be ignored completely. It is often an excellent jumping off point for the researcher and amazing as it may seem, sometimes the truth behind a particular myth is more closely tied to the myth than anyone could ever guess.

Some myths have elements of historical fact embedded in them, while others seem to be purely fanciful and have no way to be tested and proved. The myths of past civilizations have long held fascination for mankind and raised many questions. Embellishment and seemingly plausible details can creep into the history of an event, eventually rendering it legend. If enough time passes and the history is lost, this legend can turn to myth. Examples of this evolution from history to myth can be seen everywhere, even in more modern history. Two hundred years ago in American history George Washington was a living person whose deeds were well-known to the people. Centuries later the best-loved story about him, his confession of chopping down a cherry tree, is legendary, and according to scholars, most likely untrue. It is not hard to imagine that with the passage of a few more centuries or the loss of a couple key historical documents his story would be relegated to myth and if his exploits are even believed valid, they would be attributed to a group of men and not the individual. In this way even recent history is already on the path to becoming myth. How then does the student of mythology learn to tell the difference and find the kernels of truth in tales that are sometimes so improbable that the ordinary human reaction is to shrug them off as fantasy?

The question of how to determine myth from history is not a new one. In fact, modern skepticism towards myths isn't so modern. Around 300 B.C. Euhemeros of Messene assumed that his ancestors were primitives with no scientific method who exaggerated historical events.[31] This is a view many now take towards events that occurred in the era of Euhemeros.

For many years there was not much interest in testing myths for their historical content. However, there is a danger in assuming that all stories categorized as myth are just that. Oftentimes valuable truths and important archaeological discoveries can be missed or overlooked by black boxing all myths. For years archaeologists believed that the story of Troy was only a myth until it was discovered in 1873 by Heinrich Schliemann, a merchant turned archaeologist.[32] Most scientists were so busy assuming that this story couldn't have any basis in fact that no one had bothered to go looking for it. Yet Heinrich found the city, right where the Iliad said it would be. The city was actually one of several layers, cities that had been subsequently built on top of each other, but that did not take away from the fact that he read the story, went to the place that it described and found a previously lost civilization. Recently scientists researching the Svan people in the Caucasus Mountains have been finding some historical roots for the story of Jason and the Golden Fleece. Among other things, the local peoples use an ancient gold mining technique wherein they put sheepskins in the rivers when the ice begins to melt. Gold in the water sinks to the bottom of the river and is trapped in the skins. When the miners pull the fleeces up they can be completely covered in gold,

---

[31] Scott Leonard and Michael McClure, Myth and Knowing: an Introduction to World Mythology (New York: McGraw-Hill, 2004) 4.
[32] Rosenberg, Donna, World Mythology: an Anthology of the Great Myths and Epics (Lincolnwood, Illinois: NTC Publishing Group, 1999) 108.

looking exactly like a Golden Fleece and providing a plausible explanation for the prized Golden Fleece Jason and the Argonauts were seeking.[33]

Given these and other discoveries, it may behoove scientists to take a new view of mythology, seeking to find the fact behind it instead of just dismissing it out-of-hand. Unfortunately, determining what is fact and what is fiction is not an easy task for any researcher. Some myths might always baffle researchers. However, with the help of the scientific community, it is becoming increasingly possible to study what once might have seemed impossible. Many geologists today agree that there was a world-wide flood at some point in the past. Many attribute it to the thaw which followed the last great ice age. Whatever the cause, science has helped lend credence to the flood myths told by nearly every culture. With the help of geologists, archaeologists and other scientists many other myths might be proven to be based on fact. The student of mythology can help this effort by identifying specific trends in mythology across cultures. The next step is to look at specific myths and try to determine if there are any facts in them that might be proven. These may be small, seemingly insignificant facts such as what a particular type of object is used for or facts that help reshape our entire view of ancient history. In this manner other cities like Troy might be discovered and objects as mystical sounding as golden fleeces might be proven through study of the history and customs of indigenous peoples.

---

[33] Ibid., p. 161.

There is another value to mythology that makes it imperative that it not be disregarded entirely. The study of the mythology of a particular group of people can help the archaeologist understand more about the beliefs, values and moral codes of that group. The ideals of a culture are often revealed in these stories. This can be seen throughout history. Greek stories of heroes give modern readers a clue as to what character traits were valued in Greek society. Even modernly myths that espouse moral character are being created. George Washington stands as a moral figure for American society because he could not tell a lie about chopping down the cherry tree. Regardless of the historical veracity of the story, it demonstrates a greater truth that American society values honesty and tries to instill it in their children through the retelling of this story. In Japan loyalty is one of the most valued character traits. Therefore, Japanese myths such as the Kotan Utunnai promote loyalty as one of the greatest attributes. It is an attribute shared by friends and foes alike. Loyalty is an important aspect of Japanese behavior and morality that exists to this day. A culture puts its values into its myths and it also takes its identity from its myths.

Myth is powerful and whoever gets to control it and define it results in cultural and political consequences.[34] In this way, it is not unlike the "story" that archaeology seeks to uphold and continue. Truth is often subjugated in both instances. Like archaeology, the study of mythology has led to

---

[34] Leonard, p.5.

extreme cases of nationalism. The Nazis used it to justify their political machinations.[35]

Modern archaeologists are starting to take another look at mythology and ask questions about what kind of truth lies at the heart of the stories told by different cultures. This willingness to actually investigate myths and try to find the truth behind them has led to many great discoveries, including the finding of Troy. Perhaps someday many stories that are now ignored will receive greater attention and elements of them will be proven to be factual. It is arrogant to believe that there is no truth to be had in myths. Even if there is no historical fact to a particular myth, there is cultural truth. If for no other reason than to gain a greater understanding of these past cultures, mythology deserves to be studied in a serious light by archaeologists and anthropologists. It is then that mankind will truly understand its own history and the connection all cultures share with each other through common mythological themes and events. Serious study will perhaps even lead the way to discovery of some elements of shared history.

---

[35] Ibid., p 10.

Who Translated This?

Dr. Daniel Jackson - Stargate

October 21, 1931

Against all odds I had found the third and final Tear and had barely escaped France with my life. I'm not sure I'll ever be allowed to step foot in the country again which is truly a shame. Nobody likes it when you disturb the remains of the dead, but when the remains are those of a famous person people get even more touchy about it. What choice did I have, though? The tablet that Dr. Reid loaned me which discusses the Tears of Man seemed to indicate that there was some sort of time frame, a countdown that once started couldn't be stopped, that would lead to the final destruction of the island resting on the bottom of the ocean. It would have taken months, maybe years to get permission to do what I did, and maybe not even then. After all, noone but someone like me would want to disturb that body.

I can't dwell on it. I did what I had to do. Now I just have to figure out what this tablet is trying to tell me about how the tears will reveal the location of Atlantis. I am growing frustrated, though. The tablet was translated a few decades ago and I have both the tablet and the translation. It's slow work, but I'm trying to make my own translation now as the original does not seem quite adequate.

There are a few words the original translator seems to have gotten wrong or was unable to figure out altogether which leave frustrating gaps. It leads me to wonder who translated this and how could they have gotten ninety percent of it right and yet the crucial parts wrong?

I've seen it before, but it never ceases to amaze me. I wish there was someone else I could entrust this task to, but I feel I am running out of time and I'm not sure who I can trust with this.

Still, I'm not entirely without hope. The translation is coming along and I have already corrected some minor mistakes. I'm beginning to think that the answer is right in my grasp. It's as though I already know something which should be of help in this process. Something keeps tickling the back of my mind, as though demanding to be heard, but every time I try to focus on the thought it slips away like sand through my fingertips.

Sand...

I think I have an idea.

- Excerpted from the journals of Charles "Tex" Ravencroft

IN FICTION

The scenes are familiar and at the heart of them is a desperate need to be able to speak or read a different language. If you think about it you can almost hear Dr. Belloq chastising Indiana Jones because he doesn't speak Hovitos. Given that Indy speaks more than twenty languages it's almost surprising he can't speak that one. He's even fluent enough to argue in Cantonese with his sidekick, Short Round. The actor who played Short Round went on to act in an epic treasure hunting film shortly after which was beloved by a generation - *The Goonies*. There we see another example of translating as the kids struggle to translate the symbols, interpret the words, and follow the treasure map that has come into their possession.

Whether negotiating with someone from a different culture or translating a document key to either your survival or your quest, fictional archaeologists have, as a whole, been shown as quite adept and easily able to extrapolate.

Dr. Daniel Jackson can translate anything. That's one of the biggest takeaways of the *Stargate* franchise. He's so good at it that he puts other translators to shame as evidenced by the fact that in the film he scratches out one scientist's phrase of "door to heaven" and replaces it with the word stargate. Now, granted, Stargate is a much better title for the movie than Door to Heaven would be, but the differences between the two concepts at first glance can seem rather negligible. However, look at the difference more closely between "heaven" and "star". The most common meaning of the word star is a reference to the celestial bodies in the universe that we see at night as twinkling lights. Although one meaning of the word "heaven" can reference the sky, the most common use of that word references the place where souls go after people die and angels sing songs all day. Suddenly the difference between star and heaven becomes a big deal with one being a physical location and the other being a metaphysical location.

At any rate, we can all rest assured Dr. Jackson is on the job and when it comes to translating new alien languages within a matter of days or even minutes we know he's <u>never</u> wrong. Of course, he isn't the only archaeologist out there who has an almost preternatural ability to translate what he hears or sees. It is a vital skill if the TV show or film's plot is to move along.

IN OUR HEARTS

We'd like to believe that all puzzles can be solved and that two people can learn to communicate despite all odds. If there are barriers to communication we believe that it's just because the wrong person is doing the communicating. It takes a Jane Goodall to help us understand animals, a Jean-François Champollion to unlock the Rosetta Stone so we could translate ancient Egyptian, and a Reverend Thomas Hopkins Gallaudet to bring together people with different sign language systems in one place to create the standard for American Sign Language thereby facilitating modern communication. The message we hear and believe over and over again is that no puzzle can't be solved, no barrier can't be broken down, no language can't be translated.

This very belief and the thrill of being able to be the one who solves the riddle or translates the puzzle is responsible for a great deal of leisure activities. Books of games ranging from crossword puzzles to cryptography puzzles to logic puzzles are wildly popular because people feel a sense of accomplishment when they complete the puzzle, crack the code, or untangle the facts.

Translation itself is a complex process that involves more than just the manual conversion from one language to another. Yet, despite its intricacies and the potential pitfalls, we continue to champion the notion that anything is translatable no matter how impossible the task may seem or how limited the amount of data and resources to support the effort.

IN FACT

There are many types of languages, but there are only two types of archaeology, one type is aided by texts written by the culture being studied and the other is not. Text aided archaeology is archaeology that utilizes the historical record and which has recourse to ancient writings and drawings. These writings help an archaeologist understand the context of his finds and put together a clearer picture of ancient civilizations.

The development of a written language in a civilization helps to record events, communicate information, and capture ideas. Most ancient civilizations developed their own writing systems which were used by their own people and even occasionally shared with other civilizations with which they did trade. These written documents are often a great aid to archaeologists as they try to understand more about the culture and daily life of people who lived thousands of years ago. Many ancient writings have been translated, but some languages, such as the writings of the Harappan and the Indus, have yet to be deciphered.[36] Modern writing systems are descendants of these ancient ones. The ancient Phoenicians used an alphabetic script that was a predecessor to the modern alphabet.[37]

Written language was used for a number of purposes in ancient cultures. The most common use of language was to keep extensive records of trade, business transactions and even taxes paid to kings or other leaders. In this respect, as a manner of record keeping, writing was used in much the same way as it is modernly. There were also more colorful uses of language, which were common in ancient as well as modern times. One of the earliest examples of Greek inscriptions is found on the leg of a statue of Ramesses II at Abu Simbel. It was graffiti carved by a Greek man who was returning home after serving the Egyptian Pharaoh as a mercenary.[38] In this way the

[36] Christopher Scarre and Brian M. Fagan, Ancient Civilizations 2nd ed. (Upper Saddle River, New Jersey: Prentice Hill, 2003) p. 18, 162
[37] Ibid., p. 221
[38] Ibid., p. 286

Greek who carved the graffiti was not keeping records but communicating information.

The Han Empire in China standardized the writing script and used it to run the empire.[39] Bureaucrats were formally trained and candidates had to pass formal written examinations before they could begin their work.[40] Eventually it was one of these imperial officials that invented paper.[41] Like the Han Empire the Roman Empire also used the written word to help run the empire. Romans used very thin sheets of wood to write on that could actually be folded and addressed much like modern day letters.[42] In addition to using writing to keep track of food and troop movements, writing was also used in correspondence much as it is modernly. A famous letter that has been found was from the wife of one military officer to another, extending an invitation to come to her birthday party.[43] Much of ancient communication showed very little difference to modern communication.

One of the most common uses of writing in ancient societies was the writing of laws. Ur-Nammu has one of the oldest extant codes of law.[44] In Babylon a pillar has been discovered which has a law code written upon it containing 282 clauses. Among other laws it showed that women, though subordinate, could own property and divorce their husbands for

---

[39] Ibid., p. 398
[40] Ibid., p. 393
[41] Ibid., p. 398
[42] Ibid., p. 330
[43] Ibid., p. 331
[44] Ibid., p. 97

maltreatment.[45] There are countries in the modern world where this is not true even today.

Another use of writing in ancient civilizations was to capture ideas. In this way important thoughts and principles could be preserved and shared. Religions and philosophies were transcribed and shared with thousands of others right up until the modern day. Writing allowed the works of Homer and Plato to be read not only by their contemporaries but also by modern man. With an emphasis on religious matters, Maya writing and Egyptian script, though developed half a world away from each other, played a similar role in their respective societies.[46] Religions have been passed down for millennia because of the power of the written word and educated people who could write texts, read them and translate them.

The importance of ancient writings is something that has been understood for a long time. One of the earliest collections of ancient documents belonged to the Assyrian Empire. Despite their reputation as conquerors and hunters, the Assyrian kings collected clay tablets and ancient writings, putting them into libraries and creating places of learning.[47] Napoleon, a modern conqueror, understood the importance of ancient texts and because of his teams of scientists the Rosetta stone, which unlocked the key to the Egyptian language, was discovered and preserved.

Ancient writings are a great aid in piecing together the history and culture of our ancestors. They

---

[45] Ibid., p. 209
[46] Ibid., p. 421
[47] Ibid., p. 235

also present some unique challenges, though. Chief among these are problems with translation and interpretation.

One of the problems with text aided archaeology is the difficulty of translating ancient texts. Archaeologists can struggle for years to decipher a particular ancient language. Even then it takes more than hard work to translate a language that is long dead. It also takes a bit of good fortune. In the case of Egyptian hieroglyphics that good fortune came in the form of the Rosetta stone. Unfortunately such a ready tool has not yet been discovered to help with the translation of many languages. Several ancient languages have not yet been deciphered. Some of these represent the most ancient forms of writing yet discovered. This hinders the study of these cultures and their history. Only once all the ancient texts can be translated will archaeologists have a more complete picture of the culture and history of the past.

Another frequent problem is that translations are not always accurate. There are several reasons for this. Sometimes ancient symbols could have more than one meaning, or in the case of a phonetic language, more than one sound. This leads to guesswork on the part of the translator who must decide which meaning or sound is the correct one. There are not always direct correlations between the ancient language and the modern one which it is being translated into either. Without a complete sense of the ancient context, this task becomes nearly impossible. A word-for-word translation might lose the meaning of a phrase and vice-versa. Translations are also only as good as the knowledge and skill of the translator making them.

A great example of this is the Bible. There are dozens of translations currently available. Some claim to be the most linguistically accurate with a word for word translation. Others claim to be the most culturally accurate, taking into account the original meanings ascribed to certain words and phrases. This has lead to some verses having different meanings in different translations. Matthew 16:18 provides a good example of this:

> And I tell you that you are Peter, and on this rock I will build my church, and the gates of Hades will not overcome it.[48] (New International Version)

> Now I say to you that you are Peter, and upon this rock I will build my church, and all the powers of hell will not conquer it.[49] (New Living Translation)

> And I say also unto thee, That thou art Peter, and upon this rock I will build my church; and the gates of hell shall not prevail against it. (King James Version)

> And I also say to thee, that thou art a rock, and upon this rock I will build my assembly, and

---

[48] *NIV Bible*, www.biblegateway.com, (accessed July 22, 2006).
[49] *NLV*, (Tyndale House: 2004) www.biblegateway.com, (accessed July 22, 2006).

gates of Hades shall not prevail against it.
(Young's Literal Translation)

And I tell you that you are Peter. On this rock I
will build My church. The powers of hell will
not be able to have power over My church.[50]
(New Life Version)

I tell you this. You are Peter. On this rock I will
build my church. The power of death will not
destroy it.[51] (Worldwide English)

The differences between Bible translations in the
Western world and the Eastern world are particularly
dramatic. In the Western translations while on the
cross Jesus cries out "My God, why have you forsaken
me?" In Eastern translations Jesus triumphantly
proclaims "My God, My God, for this I have been
spared!"[52] This difference completely changes both
the meaning and the tone of the passage.

Given that the New Testament is only two
thousand years old and has been consistently read
since its creation, it is easy to see that much older
documents could have been mistranslated. When these
records are also written in extinct languages, the
translation problems become even more likely.

---

[50] *New Life Version*, (Christian Literature International: 1969)
www.biblegateway.com, (accessed July 22, 2006).
[51] *Worldwide English (New Testament)*, (SOON Educational Publishers)
www.biblegateway.com, (accessed July 22, 2006).
[52] Carole McDonnell, *Surprising Differences in Bible Translations Across
the World*, http://www.faithwriters.com/article-details.php?id=1720,
(accessed July 22, 2006).

Sometimes differences of only a letter or two can have a significant impact on a word. Historians can't agree on the correct spelling even for the names of some ancient writers. The Egyptian historian Manetho has had his name written as: Manethōs, Manethō, Manethos, Manēthōs, Manēthōn, and even Manethōth, Manethon, Manethonus, and Manetos.[53] In a similar fashion it has been speculated whether ancient references to Auritians and Aleteans might be actually describing Atlanteans.

The other problem with text aided archaeology is interpretation of ancient texts. Even if the translation is accurate there are no guarantees that the archaeologist will be able to interpret it correctly. Without understanding the full cultural context, it is hard to understand exactly what is meant by many phrases. The meaning of particular words can mutate over time. Also, colloquialisms cause particular difficulty. Even modernly this is a problem. Ma Petite Chou Chou, a French term of endearment is translated into English as "my little cabbage". There is no way someone could look at this and understand that it was an affectionate endearment if they didn't understand the culture and had the saying explained to them. English speakers would instead be likely to think of this as an insult.

Problems also arise when one word can have multiple meanings. The word "bear" can ultimately reference a type of an animal, be used as a description for a person, refer to a difficult task or describe the stock market. It can also be used as a verb to mean to

---

[53] *Manetho,* http://en.wikipedia.org/wiki/Manetho, (accessed July 22, 2006).

hold up, to give birth to, to support weight, to produce fruit, or to carry arms. If that didn't cause enough confusion the word "bare" is pronounced the same way and also has multiple meanings. In another example, the Hawaiian word 'aloha' can mean a variety of things including 'hello', 'goodbye,' or even 'I love you'. When dealing with a dead language the issues multiply because there are no native speakers who can help provide context or explain idiosyncrasies in the language and the meaning behind certain words and phrases.

The popular Harry Potter books provide a good modern day example of linguistic difficulties. For each book in the series, the version that is printed in Britain is different than the version that is printed in the United States. This is particularly odd given that both are English speaking countries and that the United States was a colony of the British Empire until the end of the 18th century. However, differences in the language, particularly with slang phrases, and differences in the cultures, make it difficult for the average American reader to understand some of the vocabulary in the British version of the book. Concern that American audiences would think of Greek philosophers instead of medieval alchemists even led the first book to be retitled *Harry Potter and the Sorcerer's Stone* in America as opposed to the original title *Harry Potter and the Philosopher's Stone*. These are two countries that share a common history and language and yet even with modern communications things get lost in translation. How much more difficulty must the archaeologist have in translating and interpreting the texts of cultures long since dead which bear little resemblance to his own? How much is lost in translation?

On top of these problems with translation and interpretation of ancient texts, two other difficulties face archaeologists. Sometimes the written record is sketchy at best. Even when records can be found intact the archaeologist then must ferret out the facts from the fiction.

Sometimes ancient texts have been lost in whole or in part and what we know of them comes from references by other writers. This makes it difficult to fully study a culture when only fragmentary or secondary records exist. In this way we know that the Greek writer Hellanicus had a writing entitled "Atlantis" which was written before Plato's account. Unfortunately only fragments still exist and it does not offer much help to those wishing to research Atlantis.

The other problem with written records is that archaeologists have to decide what is fact and what is fiction. While mythology is important, it can sometimes be difficult to distinguish from history. These determinations are often left to the discretion of the archaeologist who might choose to correctly or incorrectly label something as history rather than myth.

Things that can't easily be recognized as myth aren't the only things that create problems deciphering fact from fiction. There is a saying that history is written by the winners. This was as true in ancient times as it is today. In ancient Egypt battles were written about in such a way to glorify the Egyptians and give praise to the Pharaoh for the victory, regardless of whether they had actually won or lost. Rewriting the past to put a more favorable light on it is something that the archaeologist will have a more difficult time disproving the story. This means that the careful archaeologist must cast a critical eye over everything he reads, no matter how straight-forward and factual it might seem.

Translation is one of the most difficult things in the world to do and to do accurately. The popularity of the phrase "lost in translation" is evidence of this. Human beings have a very hard time translating and conveying things even when they are not converting them to another language. This is due to a variety of factors including lack of understanding, lack of appreciation of nuance, lack of memory, and even the use of wrong or confusing words.

Imagine playing a game of telephone. You get in a line with a bunch of other people. The first person whispers something into the second person's ear. The second person is supposed to whisper whatever it was verbatim into the third person's ear and so on down the line of people. Inevitably when the last person speaks it out loud to the group it has changed, often hilariously and dramatically, from what the first person actually said. The longer and more complicated the original message, the greater the chance for mutation and error.

Now imagine playing that same game, only having to pass on the message in a language different from the one you heard it in. The potential for error becomes staggering by the time you reach the end of the line and you'll be lucky to retain anything of the original.

As stated previously, we have enough trouble understanding the things we hear and read in our native language. In English you have words that sound alike even though they are spelled differently and have different meanings. In written language, particularly in communications such as emails it can be very hard to understand the tone or intent of the speaker. That's one of the reasons computer users developed the language of emoticons to help give you the same emotional context you would be able to figure out if you could see the person's body language or hear the tone of their voice. Still, even those can only carry you so far in understanding the meaning and tone behind a particular message.

The same trouble we have with these things is increased by an order of magnitude when the archaeologist is trying to translate something even when he has a base understanding of how to read the language. When dealing with previously unknown languages the problem of translating it becomes nearly insurmountable and requires a lot of patience, context from other resources, and a degree of intuition and luck.

While some people are much more geared to learning and understanding languages than others, there is still a learning curve. The translator will not always be right. Most importantly, if you're staring down a gun, knife, or spear and waiting for the archaeologist in your group to suddenly be able to pick up a new language and say the magic words that will save you, you're in for a very painful awakening.

So, You Think You've Solved in 14 Days What They Couldn't Solve in Two Years?

General West - Stargate

November 16, 1931

    I'm standing here because of a tablet and a dead man. Both of them held a key to the puzzle. My hands are shaking. I have the three Tears of Man in my possession. I am afraid, though, that something is about to happen to me. I'm stopping to scribble these words in case someone should find my body. Please send this journal and my remains to Dr. Reid [Address omitted. The journal picks up and it appears that several hours have passed.]

    ...right about so many things. I found a disc with markings on it. The three tears fit into slots on it. The disc activated. I've never seen anything like it in my life. There was an image and it spoke to me. It told me that I have this one chance to save Atlantis or it will perish for all time. Before I can, though, I must collect three more of these orichalcum gems, larger ones, that are known as the "Tears of Poseidon". As the Tears of Man tell where the city is, the Tears of Poseidon can restore it. Apparently there have been four windows of opportunity to do this throughout history, but I am the first to get this far. If I fail, the city will be lost forever. I know where I have to go to find the first Tear of Poseidon. I am only grateful that I have a chance of finding it. A few decades ago, all would have been lost. Who would have thought that the world would owe everything to one dreamer with a book?

- Excerpted from the journals of Charles "Tex" Ravencroft

IN FICTION

Indiana Jones and Daniel Jackson both can do in a matter of days what other archaeologists have spent their lives trying to accomplish. Benjamin Franklin Gates was able to accomplish what generations of his ancestors couldn't with the exact same information they had. Is it some sort of sixth sense that helps these heroes out? Do they have stronger instincts when it comes to where to look for things? Are they just standing on the shoulders of giants and lucky enough to be in the right place to make that final intuitive leap? With our fictional heroes it almost seems to be a combination of these things.

Oftentimes what sets our heroes apart is determination, imagination, outside-the-box thinking, and a fair amount of luck. Indiana Jones is a perfect paragon of all these virtues. Daniel Jackson also excelled in out of the box thinking. For Daniel, glimpsing a horoscope in a newspaper at the right time was the bit of luck that fired his imagination and helped him unlock the mysteries of the Stargate. Benjamin Gates has determination in spades when he decides that the only way to keep the Declaration of Independence safe is to steal it before someone else can. The ability to continue his treasure hunt is just a side effect that he can learn to live with.

Many fictional archaeologists happen to be in the right place at the right time. If Lara Croft had been off on another adventure or just on vacation she would have missed hearing the suddenly ticking clock that led her on the adventures of the first *Tomb Raider* film. If Max Eilerson had been on earth when the Drakh plague was unleashed he wouldn't have been able to join the crew of the Excalibur for the hunt of a lifetime in *Crusade*. The ability to receive the call to action at the right time and the willingness to spring to action are what make our fictional archaeologists great.

IN OUR HEARTS

We love to believe that someone can come in and solve a problem that is staggeringly impossible for everyone else. We'd like to believe that through intelligence, education, imagination, innovation, and luck all things are doable and that they are doable in record time. Myths about detectives who can solve nearly any crime, about mechanics who can fix nearly any machine, and whiz kids who seem to come out of nowhere abound. There's a couple of reasons for that. First, we enjoy those types of stories, love believing that an individual person is capable of greatness. Second, there are enough actual examples of people who do possess those skills and who can solve the seemingly unsolvable that we know it's possible.

As humans we're very task oriented. We complete one task and we start on another. Sometimes it can be hard to focus on long term goals that aren't readily achievable within a few hours or even weeks. It's because we're designed to want to achieve and move on to the next thing. Very few people have the patience to spend years trying to solve a single puzzle or decipher a single riddle, not without substantial progress or measurable milestones along the way. This is another reason why it's gratifying to find heroes who can do these herculean tasks in short order and move on to the next one.

Of course, another reason that our heroes of the screen can pull off these amazing feats in such a short amount of time is that trying to watch them solve something in two years instead of two weeks leads for a less exciting movie or television show. If we don't have the patience to slog through years of monotony on a problem of our own why would we have the patience to watch someone else do it? Watching them achieve something monumental in a short amount of time, however, is like watching them win the jackpot. Even if we're not the ones winning, we can still revel in the excitement of the moment alongside our heroes and cheer them on to victory.

IN FACT

People often speak of those who become an overnight success. What they don't see is that it probably took that individual years of back-breaking work to achieve that "overnight success". Howard Carter worked as an archaeologist in Egypt for three decades before his famous discovery of King Tut's tomb.

Instant success in any endeavor is rare and in archaeology it's almost unheard of. However, there are frequent breakthroughs that help advance the study sometimes by years. These quantum leaps forward can be attributed to several factors or a combination of them. Some of these can be attributed to genius, others to luck, a great many to advances in technology, and still others to inspiration.

Genius can play a role in propelling archaeological advances forward. Strokes of genius can be attributed to many of the men who helped to translate the Rosetta Stone which provided the key to finally being able to decipher hieroglyphics.

Sometimes pure luck can also advance archaeology. Such was the case with the initial discovery of the Rosetta Stone or when some Bedouin shepherds accidentally discovered the Dead Sea

Scrolls. Even still it took about a year before the scrolls came to the attention of a scientist. From there it took months and months to find the caves and the progress was hindered by the 1948 Arab-Israeli War.

Other quantum leaps in the field are facilitated by advances in technology. By necessity so much of archaeology is about interpretation and guesswork that it is vitally important that archaeologists have the best tools available to them. Sometimes the best tool is an emergent technology. High altitude radar mapping was used in 1984-1985 to discover a previously unknown people.[54] The mapping revealed a previously unknown settlement which had been buried by a volcano. Sonar also helped to relocate an Egyptian tomb that had been lost.[55] Probes are used in subsurface detection and mini TV cameras are used to look inside the earth and manmade structures.[56] This allows archaeologist to not only search inside small areas, but also to do so with a minimum of contamination and environmental impact.

As new technology develops it aids the scientist in his observations, but it should be remembered that where archaeology is concerned, technology is just the tool and not the goal. Sometimes the old methods are better or at least give the researcher something that all the lab equipment in the world won't. These older tools are timeless, such as good old fashioned reading. In this way a Viking settlement in Newfoundland was discovered because of clues in medieval texts.[57] In a

---

[54] Renfrew, p. 90.
[55] Ibid., p. 102.
[56] Ibid., p. 98.
[57] Ibid., p. 77.

similar way, Troy was discovered by a direct reading of the primary source material. In a society rushing to embrace every new technology, the serendipity of discovering something in an ancient book is slipping away from the average scientist. No equipment in the world can replace a sharp pair of eyes, a willing pair of hands, and human perseverance and intuition. All of these work together with technology, though to bring the past to life.

Inspiration can also help to advance archaeology quickly. As already discussed, it certainly played a big role in Heinrich Schliemann's discovery of Troy.

Most archaeological discoveries take years and once found they certainly take years to fully examine and evaluate all the data from them. Occasionally, though, there are breakthroughs that would make even our fictional heroes proud.

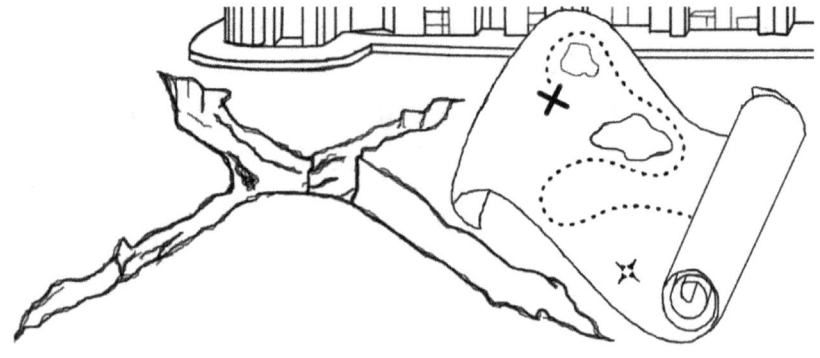

X Marks the Spot

*Dr. Henry "Indiana" Jones - Indiana Jones and the
Last Crusade*

November 26, 1931

It's Thanksgiving and I'm about as far away
from home as I could be. For the past week I've felt
like there was something dogging my footsteps,
someone or something that was trying to keep me from
my goal. Today I have become convinced this is true.
The burning of my hotel several nights ago was no
accident, but was targeted at me. Why then did the
culprit allow me to escape with my life? In the last few
years I've been stabbed, shot, burned, buried alive.
There was even an attempted drawing-and-quartering
once that I shall never forget. This is different, though.
I sense danger and menace, but I'm beginning to
suspect that whoever is behind this doesn't want me
dead, just stopped. But why? I know I should be
grateful for small miracles but time is running out and
I cannot brook delay. Fortunately, I know exactly

where I have to go. More later tonight if I'm successful.

It was there! Exactly where I thought it would be. I have to admit that it was gratifying to see the excavations at Troy in person after having read so much about them. There are several cities piled on top of each other and I found the level that everyone believes to be the ancient city. I disguised myself as one of the workers and I found my way into a temple that was only just excavated a few months ago. I'm lucky that it had been or my job would have been incredibly difficult, perhaps impossible.

I didn't know where I was supposed to look in the temple. I only knew that I was looking for a particular symbol that the disc had revealed to me which would mark the spot where the Tear of Poseidon was. I have to admit, I'm still having trouble grasping all of this, but I'm daring to believe. I spent an hour in the temple searching fruitlessly and I could hear workers getting closer to where I was. I had to hope I could find what I was looking for before I was discovered. I also worried about whoever it was that was following me and kept expecting them to make an appearance at any moment.

Finally the light from my torch illuminated a section of the wall which when looked at in just the right way resembled the symbol I was looking for. Even after everything I've seen I still feel that swell of excitement when the moment of discovery as at hand. This was no different and I practically held my breath as I stepped closer, looking.

I didn't see the Tear. For a moment I wondered if there could be more than one of these symbols carved into the wall. I finally turned aside to start exploring the possibility when a flash of light caught my eye. There, just above the symbol, not in the center of it as I had expected, was the stone, flush with the wall around it.

I had a trowel hanging from my belt and I unhooked it and wedged the tip underneath the gem. It didn't want to budge and I gritted my teeth. I would bring the whole wall down if I had to, but who knew what kind of damage that could do the excavation? Plus, it would certainly bring people running and I couldn't afford that.

I tried from another angle and the gem moved and then fell out into my hand. I felt a swell of relief as I quickly wrapped it in cloth. It was heating up faster than the smaller versions did. I shoved it in my pocket, turned to go, and came face-to-face with a man cloaked in shadow, his face covered, and a wicked looking blade in his hand.

- Excerpted from the journals of Charles "Tex" Ravencroft

IN FICTION

"X" marks the spot is a common trope in movies that have to deal with treasure hunting in one way or another. Perhaps the funniest example occurs in *Indiana Jones and the Last Crusade* when Indy finds a roman numeral ten on the floor of a library and realizes that's where he has to dig. The scene is hilarious because earlier in the movie he told a classroom of archaeology students that X never marks the spot. It's just another example of Indy teaching real archaeology while practicing fictional archaeology.

While that X was a literal X and fictional treasure maps often show an X on them to denote the location of the treasure, not all Xs are literal but more figurative. In *Raiders of the Lost Ark* the sun shining through the headpiece of the staff of Ra would illuminate the exact location on the model of the city of where the Ark of the Covenant was being kept. Once Indy did this the light marked the spot and he knew essentially where to start digging. Each time a location is definitely described or indicated that is the equivalent of putting a virtual X on it that says "look here".

IN OUR HEARTS

"X" marks the spot. That phrase is ingrained into our psyche from the time that we are children. The X always leads to buried treasure or a lost civilization or something equally fantastic. The X is always on a map of some sort which if we can just decipher it will lead us to find the most amazing things. That's great in fiction, but in reality, there are very few maps with giant Xs on them. More often there are descriptions of locations. Since we like to solve puzzles, we would like to believe that these descriptions are at least worded as riddles that must be solved. This is the case with numerous films about treasure hunting that range from *The Goonies* to *Romancing the Stone*.

IN FACT

Real life archaeologists don't have treasure maps they're looking at or a series of tantalizing clues that will lead them to their find. Most archaeology revolves around excavating different kinds of settlements that were either known or suspected to exist or even sometimes stumbled upon accidentally.

However, adding fuel to the fire of the fiction, there are some real life examples where X does indeed mark the spot. One of the obvious ones that come to mind is the discovery of Troy where the description in the Iliad was all that was needed to give enough of a location for the excavation to commence.

Two problems exist with these virtual Xs, though. The first revolves around people not believing the veracity of the information and the second being that X no longer means what it did when the description or instructions were originally recorded.

Sometimes people know where X is but don't actually bother giving that data enough credence to put a shovel in the ground and start digging. While there could be a number of reasons for this failure to act upon the information, many times this happens when archaeologists discount the mythology of a people entirely. As discussed in a previous chapter this is a dangerous attitude to take.

Another huge problem comes with the fact that sometimes an archaeologist might know or have a very good idea where X is supposed to be, but because of changed nomenclature and landmarks it doesn't help him any. This is part of the problem with the search for the mythical Atlantis.

However, if the city existed, all may not be lost in the search for it. Other archaeologists have utilized skill, intuition, and a healthy dose of luck to help them find other ancient civilizations that were similarly lost even when the descriptions of their locations were confused, inaccurate, or made meaningless by the changing of landmarks and coastlines.

Actually, the idea that a city can be lost and traces of it not found for a lengthy period of time is not that far-fetched. For many years archaeologists have been looking for the port city of Muziris in India. The port had gained something of mythical status despite the fact that it was a well documented center of trade between India and Rome during the Roman empire.[58] Despite a description of its location in Roman documents and clues to its whereabouts in Indian writings, evidence couldn't be found for the city's existence until now. Archaeologists believe that the small town of Pattanam is where the port was. A horde of Roman coins was found a few miles away and beads and pottery have been found in the area.

[58] *Search for India's Ancient City*, June 11, 2006, BBC News, http://news.bbc.co.uk/go/pr/fr/-/2/hi/south_asia/4970452.stm, (accessed July 21, 2006).

This was a well-documented trading port from the 1ˢᵗ century B.C. through the 1ˢᵗ century A.D. Yet, it was lost for hundreds of years until its existence was questioned. Even now two questions remain: how did the city disappear and when did they cease trade with Rome? No one knows how the city disappeared and even when is vigorously questioned. Originally it was believed that trade only lasted through the 1ˢᵗ century A.D. Now some evidence seems to point to its being an active trading port into the 6ᵗʰ or 7ᵗʰ century. This is believed even though a sixth century Greek writer wrote about the trade along the Indian coast but did not mention the city of Muziris.[59]

It is astounding that an important trade port which was well documented in Roman times could disappear completely until it was almost believed to be a myth. It also makes it easier to believe that a civilization which was around thousands of years before the Roman empire, in a time before most people kept any kind of written records, could have also disappeared and become myth. If it has taken archaeologists who are actively searching this long to find evidence of a city lost a little more than a millennia ago, how long might it take archaeologists actively looking for artifacts of Atlantis to find them, given that Atlantis disappeared more than eleven millennia ago?

The discovery of Muziris is not the only discovery that makes the researcher stop and think. In 2002 a lost city was found sunken off the coast of India.[60] The ruins of the city cover many square

---

[59] Id.

kilometers. They were discovered after an exploration of the Indian myth of the Seven Pagodas and talks with local fishermen.

> The myths of Mahabalipuram were first set down in writing by British [traveler] J Goldingham, who visited the South Indian coastal town in 1798, at which time it was known to sailors as the Seven Pagodas. The myths speak of six temples submerged beneath the waves with the seventh temple still standing on the seashore. The myths also state that a large city which once stood on the site was so beautiful the gods became jealous and sent a flood that swallowed it up entirely in a single day.[61]

Scientists speculate that the city was submerged after the last ice age and is over five thousand years old. Without looking to mythology, this city might never have been found. It is scientists who are willing to suspend disbelief and go against popular opinion long enough to look for the facts of a story that are the true heroes of archaeology.

There is a third city that has been discovered within the last few years off the coast of India. In January 2002 it was announced that a sunken city had been found in the Gulf of Cambay which predated the

---

[60] *Lost City Found off Indian Coast*, April 11, 2002, BBC News, http://news.bbc.co.uk/2/hi/south_asia/1923794.stm, (accessed July 21, 2006).
[61] Id.

Harappan civilization. The city measured five miles long and two miles wide.[62] "Debris recovered from the site - including construction material, pottery, sections of walls, beads, sculpture and human bones and teeth has been carbon dated and found to be nearly 9,500 years old."[63]

In South America remains of an ancient temple and other structures were discovered in the year 2000, not underneath the ocean, but submerged in Lake Titicaca. The Incas regarded the lake as the birthplace of their civilization and many legends surround it, including one of an underwater city called Wanaku.[64]

The ocean is the first place archaeologists should turn to look for Atlantis, but as we are learning, not all sunken cities remained sunken. Landmarks and coastlines change and this makes it hard sometimes to identify the exact location of ancient sites. Ships have been found inland where there are no oceans or rivers, and now even a sunken city has been found, not beneath the ocean surface, but inland. In the year 2000 archaeologists discovered the ancient Greek city of Helike. "Classical texts suggest that all its inhabitants perished when the city sank beneath the waves after suffering a disastrous combination of earthquake and tidal wave."[65]

---

[62] *Lost City 'Could Rewrite History'*, January 19, 2002, BBC News, http://news.bbc.co.uk/2/hi/south_asia/1768109.stm, (accessed July 21, 2006).
[63] Id.
[64] *Ancient Temple Found Under Lake Titicaca*, August 23, 2000, BBC News, http://news.bbc.co.uk/2/hi/americas/892616.stm, (accessed July 21, 2006).
[65] *Archaeologists Probe Legendary City*, October 19, 2000, BBC News, http://news.bbc.co.uk/2/hi/europe/978885.stm, (accessed July 21, 2006).

Writers like Pausanias and Ovid claimed that even centuries after the disaster, the ruins of the city could still be seen beneath the waves. Modernly archaeologists spent four decades searching for the city until they began to believe that it was a myth and had never really existed. That's when some out-of-the-box thinking came into play. When searchers finally turned inland, they found the ruins of part of the city underneath a vineyard. The walls and artifacts found bore the evidence that before being buried beneath the land and trees, they had been submerged beneath water. Archaeologists discovered

> archaic walls, classical ceramic fragments and, perhaps most significantly, evidence that the ruins had been submerged beneath the sea. "We uncovered archaic walls buried in clay containing sea shells," said one of the researchers, Dr Steven Soter from the American Museum of Natural History. Dr Soter told BBC News Online that the area was resettled in the centuries following the catastrophe after the ruins became buried under river sediments.[66]

Sometimes even when we believe we have a clear X marking the spot, X isn't where we thought it was. That doesn't mean that researchers should give up the hunt for lost cities, ships, and other finds that we have some evidence for the existence or location

---

[66] Id.

of. It just means that a little more work, research, sweat and perhaps even creativity is required to find that which has been buried.

Snakes, Why Did it Have to be Snakes?

Dr. Henry "Indiana" Jones - Raiders of the Lost Ark

January 11, 1932

Sharks, why did it have to be sharks? I hate those things. Cold, dead eyes staring at you, rows of razor like teeth. It took me nearly an hour to get the bleeding in my leg to stop completely. There's going to be some serious scars left behind, but they'll be worth it. I've found the third Tear of Poseidon. Now I just need to get to Atlantis in time to resurrect the city.

Of course, that's going to mean another underwater dive and I'm dreading it. I'm in no shape to handle it in my current state, but hopefully by the time I get there I'll be better.

I nearly drowned. I'm trying not to think about that. In many ways that's worse than thinking about the sharks. Sharks can be overcome, killed. Lack of oxygen and the crushing power of the water above you? Not so easy to overcome.

Truth be told the nightmares are going to be a lot harder to live with than the scars. I'm not looking forward to going to sleep tonight which is why it's nearly midnight and I'm still awake.

That's what I keep telling myself it is. I don't want to relieve this day in my dreams. The fact that I can't sleep, don't want to sleep has nothing to do with *her*. Or what today represents.

- Excerpted from the journals of Charles "Tex" Ravencroft

IN FICTION

Mother Nature and her children are a force to be reckoned with and this is rarely more apparent than in stories about archaeologists. Indiana Jones has faced down snakes, bugs, rats, and scorpions. He and countless other adventurers have hacked their way through jungles fraught with peril from giant spiders and human enemies as well. He has survived raging rivers, eaten food that would make most people sick, and even crossed ancient rope bridges over terrifying drops that were unsteady and rotting before he purposely destroyed them.

Most fictional archaeologists and treasure hunters have to brave the wrath of mother nature in one form or another. Benjamin Franklin Gates had to survive the freezing cold of the arctic after being betrayed at the beginning of *National Treasure*. Lara Croft has to survive an earthquake in *Lara Croft Tomb*

Raider: The Cradle of Life. These are just taken in stride as part of the trials they have to endure in order to complete their quest.

IN OUR HEARTS

We've all seen a structure that Mother Nature has begun the process of reclaiming. If you leave a building alone for a long enough period of time, nature begins to reclaim it. Whether it's an abandoned house, factory, or church, the ravages of time begin to return the manmade structure to a natural state. It usually starts with something like excess weeds growing on the property. Left unchecked they will eventually begin growing through cracks in seemingly solid objects.

Pests including insects and rodents begin to take over once the human occupants are gone. These are often followed by larger mammals such as cats, raccoons, or other creatures looking for shelter.

Slowly things begin to decay. Wood rots, concrete cracks, and the structure begins to literally fall apart as more and more plants and animals move in and the elements including wind, rain, and sun take their toll. Before too many years have passed it is completely unsalvageable and well on its way to becoming forgotten ruins. If this process is happening in a tropical environment or on the edge of a forest the process is greatly accelerated.

Instinct tells us that these places are unsafe to explore even if they are fascinating. Snakes and other poisonous creatures can lurk in the tall grass. Rotted out floors can collapse beneath our weight. Rusty nails and other items lurk about threatening us with a trip to the doctor's office to get a tetanus shot. We know that dangers abound and so it is simple to believe that Indy could be suddenly confronted with a roomful of the creatures that he dreads the most. Throw in an alien landscape such as the ones Dr. Jackson frequents and who knows what kind of dangers lurk.

These types of danger-filled scenes are particularly compelling because they often depict the main characters coming face-to-face with things we ourselves fear. While many of us will never encounter sword wielding bad guys like Indy many of us have had encounters or the potential for encounters with these more natural dangers.

Most of us have seen snakes and other poisonous creatures in zoos if not out in the wild. There are countless stories about these and other unwanted intruders invading people's homes.

Most of us have stood someplace high, the edge of a cliff, a bridge, or even a manmade structure where we had the unsettling knowledge that if we somehow fell it would kill us. We understand the inherent danger in falling.

We've all been sick and disease claims lives every year. We get vaccinations as kids and make sure our pets get shots as well. Traveling to some foreign countries requires vaccination. Death by an exotic disease is also a risk that we well understand.

Finally, natural disasters like fire, flood, earthquakes and storms are also dangers that can hit very close to home. When we see fictional characters encountering these things we can sympathize easily with the danger that they're in.

All these types of dangers are common to the human experience and make for compelling stories. Plus, given the remote, desolate, and exotic locations that fictional archaeologists travel to it is easy to believe that all of these dangers and more are awaiting them. This is one area where fictional and real archaeology share a lot in common.

IN FACT

Real life archaeologists face a host of dangers in the field. These dangers fall into three main categories: nature, accidents, and man-made.

Mother Nature can indeed be a harsh mistress. Weather, animals, and treacherous terrain all present very real dangers to archaeologists in the field.

Weather can provide many challenges for archaeologists. While some dig sites are situated in places where work can continue year-round, many are not. In fact, many dig sites are in places where extremes of temperature become an issue. Inclement weather can not only halt work but can also threaten the site. Weather can also pose a problem to the people working at the site. Dehydration, sunstroke, and frostbite can all become very real problems for the workers with dangerous, potentially even fatal, consequences.

Animal threats are another fact of life for archaeologists working in the field. Spiders and poisonous insects abound all over the world. When digging in the dirt there's no telling what you might encounter. In an interview for National Geographic archaeologist Victor Thompson revealed that his worst day in the field was when his wife was bitten by a pygmy rattlesnake.[67] Dr. Herman Smith has documented a couple of very frightening encounters by himself and other members of his team with snakes of all sorts.[68] Depending on where the dig is located there might be other predators to worry about as well. A few years ago an archaeologist was attacked by a polar bear in Greenland and was badly injured but survived the experience.[69] Underwater archaeologists have to take care to make sure they're not putting themselves in danger from sharks and other sea creatures. These threats are very real and affect archaeologists.

Difficult or treacherous terrain is another danger facing archaeologists. Many dig sites are located in dangerous to access locations such as caves high in cliff faces, underwater shipwrecks, and crumbling ruins. Great care must be taken both in reaching the excavation site and in maneuvering around it.

---

[67] "Victor Thompson", National Geographic, http://www.nationalgeographic.com/explorers/bios/victor-thompson/ accessed May 9, 2013.

[68] Smith, Dr. Herman, Dig It, "Occupational Hazards for Archeologists - Snakes" http://ambergriscaye.com/museum/digit21.html accessed May 9, 2013.

[69] "Archaeologist survives polar bear attack in Greenland", August 4, 2010, http://news.monstersandcritics.com/europe/news/article_1575466.php/Archa eologist-survives-polar-bear-attack-in-Greenland accessed May 9, 2013.

Accidents can happen anywhere. There are a lot of sharp tools and other dangers present at an excavation site. Even the open pits of an excavation can provide danger. Ehud Netzer, the Israeli archaeologist who discovered the tomb of the Biblical King Herod, was killed in 2010 when a railing gave way at the Herodium archaeological site and he fell.[70] This is not the only tragic story of its kind.

Besides nature and accidents archaeologists are often put in harm's way by other people. Dangerous locals and unstable political regimes can make for very hostile work environments. Archaeologists have been kidnapped and even murdered. Albert Glock was one such archaeologist, murdered in Palestine in 1992. Incidents like these serve to remind that while real archaeologists aren't in harm's way every day like fictional ones are, they still face the same types of dangers, and, unlike their screen counterparts, they don't always get a happy ending.

---

[70] "Israeli archaeologist dies after fall at King Herod dig", BBC, October 29, 2010, http://www.bbc.co.uk/news/world-middle-east-11655704, accessed May 9, 2013.

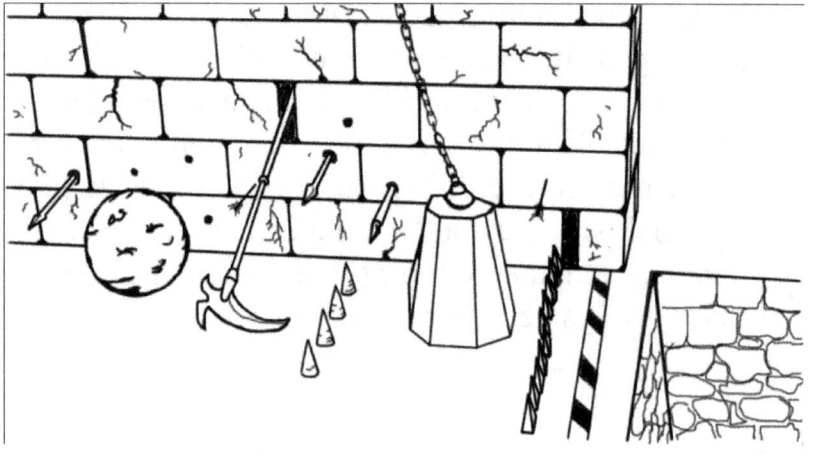

Devices of Such Lethal Cunning

Dr. Henry Jones, Sr. – Indiana Jones and the Last Crusade

January 30, 1932

I'm going to die in here, I know it. I don't see a way around that at this point and I have to accept it so that I can move forward and try to do something with the time that I have left to me. I have found a safe place for a minute where I can hide and catch my breath. I need to think, clear my head. I've been reading over all my notes from the last several months, everything I've learned, hoping that it will somehow help me survive the remaining booby traps that surely exist.

At least my shadowy adversary is no longer following me, hindering me, sabotaging my efforts. That is one of the few things that gives me the strength and the courage to press on. The trials are monumental. Both men who accompanied me here are now dead and if I'm not careful I will end up just like them. They were good men both and did not deserve to end up as they did. I cannot think of that now, though, I must only think of what I have to do next.

I have encountered arrows that fly on their own before, same with the spikes set in the ground and the poisonous gases that can be released when some chambers are opened. I have never before encountered traps of such fiendish cleverness as I have found here, though.

It is more than just the twisted nature of the minds behind them, it is also the technological sophistication that surpasses anything I have ever known. I am outmatched, outwitted, and I fear I shall not survive the next one.

I am under no delusions that if I fail my body will be buried forever with this lost city and this journal along with it. No one will know what I have found or what I gave my life for. That brings me sorrow, but it will not deter me from my cause. I must keep on writing to help myself think, to clear my mind of the fear I am feeling even as I work on trying to understand what more I might be faced with. Only with a clear mind and a steady hand will I have any prayer of making it out of this alive.

Whatever comes, though, I must press on. There's no time to go back and so I can only now save myself by going forward.

- Excerpted from the journals of Charles "Tex" Ravencroft

IN FICTION

In fiction what treasure of any real worth comes without booby traps? While these traps come in all shapes and sizes, perhaps the most iconic is the massive rolling boulder that threatens to crush Indy at the beginning of *Raiders of the Lost Ark*. Dozens of other equally devilish traps await him and others of his brothers and sisters in the fraternity of fictional adventurers. Some traps require physical agility, skill, and luck to negotiate. Others like the ones in *Indiana Jones and the Last Crusade* require the archaeologist to think their way through them and to be willing to put absolute faith in themselves and whatever is guiding them forward.

All these traps, fantastic as they may be, are designed to keep looters away and ensure that only those who are chosen or worthy can reach the treasure they are guarding. In *Stargate SG-1* the team encounters a trap called Thor's Hammer designed to destroy Goa'uld.

Traps range from the simple to the elaborate, low tech to high tech. Arrows and spears that shoot out of walls or up from floors have become a staple of the genre. Some films get more elaborate and creative with things like the leviathans that guard the sunken city in *Atlantis: the Lost Empire*. Either way booby traps are one of the most iconic and integral part of these types of stories.

IN OUR HEARTS

Even though most people dream of striking it rich, most also understand that nothing in this world comes for free. To achieve big things either an incredible amount of labor must be involved or an incredible amount of risk. In a casino those who seek treasure are gambling with their own money. Same for those who play the stock market. In the deepest jungle or the heart of a pyramid those who seek treasure are gambling with their very lives. The risk is as great as the hoped for reward.

We know the risks of treasure hunting in the real world. The greatest one is wasting untold amounts of time and money and coming up empty-handed. Another likely one is getting in trouble for trespassing or some other legal entanglements that we get ourselves into when we go trying to dig up land that doesn't belong to us. The most extreme risk, of course, is injury or death. These can be caused by either unsafe conditions where we are exploring, accidents, or irate land owners. In the end not everyone has the cash or time to risk and very few would risk death. We love watching our fictional heroes do that very thing, though. That's why we cheer them on through every trial they face, every trap they escape. We want them to win and we understand that for them to win big they are risking big.

This balance between risk and reward is so ingrained in our psyches that it can even create its own myths and urban legends. After the opening of King Tut's tomb rumors were circulated that there was a curse on it that caused those who had taken part in it to die prematurely. Those rumors are still widely believed today although scientists have debunked it by comparing the average life spans and causes of death of those who entered the tomb with those who didn't. Still, the idea of a curse whether it be a mystical one or some sort of germs or spores in the air makes sense to us and is easy to believe because it makes sense that danger would accompany the discovery of something so fabulous. In fact it almost seems like an affront to our view of the way the world works that there wasn't some sort of greater risk involved. When you realize that many Egyptian tombs either had curses spoken over them by a priest or even carved into the stone the imagination begins to have a field day.

IN FACT

In reality archaeologists are far more likely to encounter environmental hazards than booby traps when excavating a site. That's not because there isn't anything valuable to find, but generally when there is those who buried it went to great lengths to hide it as the best means of protection.

When Hawaiian royalty died, they were buried in caves in cliff faces along with their treasures. Since there are hundreds, perhaps thousands, of caves and they are only accessible for the most part by being lowered down by rope, one or two men would be responsible for choosing the cave and interring the body along with its treasures. Then, to ensure that others couldn't find and loot the cave, the ropes were cut and the workers would plunge to their death. Even ancient man knew that dead men tell no tales.

When it wasn't possible to hide the entire burial location some, like the ancient pharaohs, at least tried to make the tombs difficult to access. Some Egyptian tombs contain mazes, large stone slabs meant to block the way to the burial chamber, mounds of rubble, and inner sealed chambers all designed to keep the grave robber away from the mummy and its riches.

While most burial sites didn't have booby traps, there are exceptions that fire the imagination. Some Egyptian tombs contained trap doors, collapsing portions of floor, and even thin bits of razor sharp wire designed to decapitate intruders.[71] In China the Qin Shi Huang Mausoleum was equipped with arrows that would fire automatically at intruders.[72]

Ironically giant stone balls like those depicted in *Raiders of the Lost Ark* were discovered decades ago in Costa Rica. However, they appear to have no connection to any kind of trap mechanisms. There were many balls discovered and some of them were quite small, like the size of a child's ball and others were massive, standing taller than a man. Many have been placed in varying geometric patterns. Study of the balls and what their purpose might have been continues.

---

[71] "Curses of the Ancient Pharaohs", http://tombsofancientegypt.com/curses.html, accessed May 11, 2013.
[72] "Qin Shi Huang Mausoleum", Travel China Guide, http://www.travelchinaguide.com/attraction/shaanxi/xian/terra_cotta_army/mausoleum_1.htm, accessed May 11, 2013.

While there is more to fear from natural dangers than booby traps, these traps were not completely unheard of. Of course, like most things, the movies make every danger larger than life.

Fortune and Glory

Dr. Henry "Indiana" Jones - Indiana Jones and the Temple of Doom

March 17, 1932

I was released from the hospital today. I can finally be alone to think about everything that happened. I found Atlantis. That still seems so unbelievable, but it's true. My nine month quest is finally at an end, but it will take me years to fully understand everything that has transpired.

Everything I thought I knew about the world, about history, has been challenged and I'm only now beginning to comprehend just how much I don't know.

I found the most marvelous treasures in the heart of Atlantis. Gold and jewels and mines and weapons and knowledge. It would take a lifetime to catalogue it all. It makes me sad whenever I think that that's not my job.

There will be other finds, who knows, maybe some will be even more glorious, though I doubt it. For a man like me there will always be more work, too. Museums are always in need of people like me, whether they want to admit it or not.

I will heal and I will press on with my work. That much is certain.

But for now...I have to see a particular man about an artifact.

- Excerpted from the journals of Charles "Tex" Ravencroft

IN FICTION

"Fortune and glory" was a phrase uttered by Indiana Jones in his second film and it perfectly summed up what fictional archaeology is all about. Unless, of course, you're Daniel Jackson from *Stargate* muttering "I'm never going to get paid." Still, Daniel was on the cusp of solving one of the biggest mysteries of all time and unlocking the secret to travel between worlds. So, even if he wasn't getting paid he sure was on the verge of a lot of fame, at least, among those with the security clearance to know about it. Poor Indiana might have been going after that fortune and glory but he also seemed to keep coming up short with his major treasures either lost, returned to their proper home, or hidden away in government warehouses.

Some archaeologists have it a bit better. Benjamin Gates managed to get millions of dollars and credit for the discovery for himself and his family in *National Treasure*. Milo in *Atlantis: the Lost Empire* didn't exactly get fame and fortune, but he got the girl of his dreams. Presumably if the crew of *Crusade* had been able to complete their mission (instead of having their show canceled) Max would have received great glory and probably great fortune for being one of the people to save the entire population of Earth.

Fortune and glory are often associated with fictional archaeologists and their treasure hunting cousins. That's because they are always going after the big mysteries. The mythical Holy Grail, King Solomon's mines, discovering the creators of the pyramids, and saving the world from almost inconceivable dangers are just some of those big mysteries that our heroes find themselves in the middle of. Of course, not all the explorers in the films and television are as scrupulous as our heroes. They don't care how they come about their fortune and glory, even if it means working for the Nazis to find the Ark of the Covenant or trading treasures like the Cross of Coronado on the black market.

IN OUR HEARTS

It seems almost useless to think about buried treasure without also thinking about the fame and fortune that would surely accompany finding such a thing. The two go hand-in-hand. It's also hard to imagine finding something of great historical or cultural significance like the Ark of the Covenant without at least becoming really famous for it. Then, of course, you could sell your story for millions and see your favorite actor playing you up on the big screen. It's a wonderful dream, and far more fulfilling than the thought of having our discovery whisked away, locked up, and all mention of its discovery redacted from official documents.

We believe that people should be rewarded for the work that they do. When that work requires a great deal of risk and the ability to do what others cannot then the reward is higher. Thanks in most part to the exploits of fictional archaeologists there are a great many misconceptions about the work of real archaeologists because people want to believe that the job is that exciting so that they can live vicariously through it.

IN FACT

Daniel's lament of "I'm never going to get paid" is unfortunately a very common one for the average archaeologist. Many find that struggling to obtain grant money to continue their work is a fundamental part of the job. Even places like Hawaii where by law any digging in the ground (yes, even to install a new manhole cover downtown) automatically triggers an archaeological report are still very susceptible to economic pressures. If times are hard and fewer people are building new homes, putting in swimming pools, or expanding their septic systems then there is no steady, paying work to be had. In fact the recession of the last several years put several companies, some of them that had been around for decades, out of business. Archaeology is unfortunately one of those things that is seen as expendable when times are tough.

Of course, though the vast majority of archaeologists work in conjunction with universities or firms doing Conservation Resource Management, there are still some mavericks making a go of it alone. There are also some incredible success stories for archaeologists and treasure hunters that help reinforce the notion that this is a path to the kind of fortune and glory showcased on the big screen.

The discoveries of King Tut's tomb and Troy are well-known ones of great success that benefitted those involved. An even more modern example, though, took place in Florida. On July 20, 1985 after years of searching Mel Fisher finally found the sunken remains of the Nuestra Senora de Atocha, a Spanish ship off the coast of Florida that had gone down with stacks of silver bars, silver coins, gold, and jewels. This was not his first discovery of sunken treasure, but it was by far his greatest. The man found tens of millions of dollars worth of treasure and a museum was opened to display many recovered artifacts to the world. It has been deemed the richest discovery since the opening of King Tut's tomb. He truly lived the dream of adventurers and dreamers the world over.

Sadly, the average archaeologist does not spend his day looking for holy relics and treasure troves. He must be content with anonymity. He must understand that the enrichment of the human experience, increased knowledge, and the rediscovery of lessons that might benefit current and future society are the real prizes.

What has been discovered so far is in and of itself its own kind of fortune and glory.

One of the most astonishing discoveries of all is the fact that we are more alike our ancient ancestors than we are different. We all have the same basic needs and desires and throughout history have found remarkably similar ways to fulfill those needs and desires. Four areas that stand out are: architecture and engineering, relationships with other cultures, arts and entertainment, and the need for heroes.

When we think about the architecture and structures built by our ancestors we think about shelters such as homes, public meeting places, churches and tombs. One of the more surprising things about the architecture in ancient societies is that it wasn't just inspired by religious views or funerary needs, it also served to bring enjoyment. The Roman Emperor Nero had a ceiling in his palace that could shower perfume and flower petals down on its guests.[73] Modernly it has become a trend with theme park giants like Disney to create theater attractions that actually involve the audience in the story by spraying different smells in the air and even showering the theater patrons with water or bubbles.

Along with advances in architecture, ancient civilizations made great advances in engineering that have only recently been duplicated. The Assyrians created canals and stone aqueducts in the 600s B.C. in order to water extensive gardens and orchards. They even created screw pumps that lifted water to the top

---

[73] Christopher Scarre and Brian M. Fagan, <u>Ancient Civilizations 2nd ed.</u> (Upper Saddle River, New Jersey: Prentice Hill, 2003) 312

of the gardens where it then ran down in channels and waterfalls. The screws used were invented in Mesopotamia long before Archimedes, whom the screw was later named after, was born.[74] In Southeast Asia a drainage and transport system that transformed barren swamps into rich agricultural land was developed.[75] In addition to being warriors, the Mycenaens who took over Minoan Crete in 1450 B.C. were engineers who built dams, canals and roads.[76]

Advances in technology also benefited travel. Mail riders taking the Roman roads and changing horses could cover up to a 150 miles a day.[77] Perhaps not until the American pony express was the use of roads and relay horses used to similar advantage and able to cover as much territory. Roads were also developed in South America so that travelers could cross above swamp lands and travel between cities. In desert regions the domestication of beasts of burden, coupled with the creation of better saddles enabled travelers to use camels to cross the vast wastelands faster and with more cargo. Societies with access to navigable riverways and oceans made improvements in the structure of their boats. They also studied the weather patterns which led to improvements in sailing. These improvements in the speed and safety of travel allowed states to govern large territories. It also allowed civilizations to trade with one another more readily.

---

[74] Ibid., p. 235
[75] Ibid., p. 367
[76] Ibid., p. 264
[77] Ibid., p. 317

Advances in technology helped people in ancient civilizations create common conveniences that are remarkably similar to those enjoyed today. In Ancient Mesopotamia icehouses were constructed.[78] Technology like this wasn't in widespread use for centuries. The bathroom in the living quarters of the Minoan Knossos had a toilet with a wooden seat that discharged into a drain and had the ability to flush.[79] Less than a century ago there were great portions of civilized countries that didn't have something so advanced. Just as technological advances sprang into being all across ancient civilizations, many were also extinguished just as quickly. Many more technologies were preserved, though, perhaps because the knowledge was not held by a single group of people, but shared across cultures.

While some ancient cultures were isolated, archaeologists are discovering increasing evidence of contact between many ancient civilizations. This contact came in many forms, including: trade and commerce, wars and treaties, and colonization.

Trade and commerce were fairly common among early civilizations. Around 2100 B.C. the Minoans traded as far away as Egypt.[80] Cities often traded with other cities. When dealing with local rural communities, however, cities often raided them, taking the food and goods they wished instead of establishing trade with them.[81] Between each other cities traded luxury items as well as more everyday goods. The

---

[78] Ibid., p. 206
[79] Ibid., p. 255
[80] Ibid., p. 258
[81] Ibid., p. 10

specialization of the labor force into craftsmen guaranteed that each civilization had something unique in the way of arts, textiles, or tools. Even things that were common to both cities could have slight variations in one city that would prove valuable to others. For example, the ancient city of Brak was noted as a place to buy a particular variety of mule which was very expensive.[82] In ancient Egypt the wife of a worker placed offerings in his grave consisting of 14 different types of beer and cakes.[83] It is amazing that this type of diversity in things as simple as food and drink existed and that it wasn't reserved only for the wealthy. It is equally amazing that men would travel great distances to buy a special variety of mule in a far-away city because they believed it to be more desirable than their own local varieties. Trade wasn't only limited to goods and property. Young Greek men traveled to Egypt where they would sell their services as mercenaries to the Pharaohs.[84]

Establishment of trade with other civilizations led to development of tools to facilitate that trade. In South Asia the Harappan developed a standard weight system in an effort to reinforce their trading monopolies.[85] This weight system was adopted by other cultures and was even in use on the Island of Bahrain in the Near East.[86] The Romans used three types of coins: gold, silver and bronze[87] in order to

---

[82] Ibid., p. 92
[83] Ibid., p. 129
[84] Ibid., p. 286
[85] Ibid., p. 154
[86] Ibid., p. 205
[87] Ibid., p. 329

standardize prices for trade within the empire and without.

Interaction between ancient civilizations was not limited to trade but just as today also encompassed politics. Cities and states formed alliances with each other, waged war and made treaties. These political maneuverings were the act of civilizations to whom autonomy was a reality and expansion was desirable. To the people of Mesoamerica, warfare was a way of life promulgated by ambition and religious beliefs. Prisoners were sacrificed in religious rituals. These were not the only people who let religion and superstition dictate their warfare. An eclipse postponed a battle between Media and Lydia and the rulers took it as a sign and forged peace instead.[88] Like many Mesoamerican civilizations, the Egyptians also conquered many neighbors but used them as a source of tribute and slave labor instead of sacrifices to the gods. Some societies chose an alternative empire expanding method over warfare: colonization

Colonization was used by many civilizations to expand their power base, give themselves a foothold in other areas, and provide a new source of commerce. By the 8th century B.C. the Phoenicians had established overseas colonies as far away as Spain, North Africa and Sicily.[89] Greek civilization included colonization. One of the cities created by the Greeks was Massilia in southern France which is the modern day city of Marseilles.[90] Colonization as an empire

---

[88] Ibid., p. 240
[89] Ibid., p. 227
[90] Ibid., p. 279

building tactic remained an active part of the political scene into modern times.

Another interesting discovery about ancient civilizations is the investment of time and money into arts and entertainment to occupy, inspire and amuse the population. Division of labor ensures that there are craftsmen whose job is to create works of beauty that inspire others and demonstrate wealth or position of the owners. Division of labor also allows a civilization to enjoy more free time which can be filled with amusements and diversions. Art and entertainment are not only demonstrative of a society or an individual's status but also indicative of the level of freedom in the lives of the individuals. In modern society art is meant to inspire and indicate status and entertainment is meant to be a diversion. The same was true in ancient societies.

Art has long been used to inspire people and engender a sense of wonder and awe. Some of the most elaborate displays of architectural art are associated with temples, palaces and tombs. The Assyrians built gardens and orchards in Ninevah that are likely the famous hanging gardens of Babylon.[91] In ancient Greece elaborate temples were created to the gods but the act of creating them was for the good of the people. The temples were a source of civic pride and inspiration. They inspired the populace to create great works of art, to explore philosophy and to feel loyalty toward their cities.

Art has always been a symbol of a person's status. In ancient times only the very rich could afford

---

[91] Ibid., p. 235

it. Even in modern day Russia tiny hand-painted boxes are valued at an average cost of a month's salary and are therefore beyond the reach of the average working class man. Great kings and modern rulers commission works of art to showcase their wealth and demonstrate some positive aspect of their personality. Leaders of most ancient civilizations were buried with vast riches in order to show their prestige and often as something to accompany them into the afterlife. Just as the status of an individual can be demonstrated by the amount of disposable wealth and luxuries he enjoys, the status of a city or state can also be seen by the amount of art and other riches it compiles into public museums.

The need to be entertained is a very human one and evidence of it can be found in the ancient past as well as modern day. Modern theater goers pay exorbitant prices to be entertained and tickets for popular concerts, sports events, Broadway shows, and exclusive movie premiers are nearly worth their weight in gold. Entire industries have developed around bringing entertainment to the people whether it's in a movie theater or a circus big top. The trend for people to place such a high value on entertainment and spectacle is anything but new. Entertainment has long been used as a diversion and a bonding experience.

In ancient Egypt a dancing dwarf from Nubia caused Pharaoh far more excitement than all the riches brought to him.[92] Spectators at the Roman Coliseum demanded a high price for their entertainment – blood.

---

[92] Ibid., p. 343

The blood of thousands of men and animals was spilled to keep the people entertained. Evidence of ancient game boards has even been found inside burial mounds. Entertainment distracts people and lets them focus on something fun, especially when their lives are hard and tedious. The ancient rulers understood this as well or better than the modern ones. The Roman emperors knew that spectacles in the Coliseum kept the people from growing restless and revolting against them. For the Mayans the threat of becoming a human sacrifice was an everyday reality. Yet they took this potentially stressful element of life and turned it into play. They developed a ball game with deeply religious significance. The losers were sacrificed.[93] Few modern day athletes would agree to compete under such circumstances but to the Maya it was a part of life and the game gave them much needed pleasure.

Entertainment also gave the viewers a sense of fraternity, of belonging to something larger than themselves. The same sort of camaraderie can be found today when people cheer together for their favorite soccer team or stand in line together for hours waiting to see the latest film. Enjoyed pleasure creates a bond between people and gives them a sense of loyalty to each other and to the provider of the entertainment. This loyalty worked to the advantage of ancient rulers who strove to keep the people happy, satisfied, connected to one another and grateful to the ruler for providing the entertainment. The ability to establish elaborate entertainments and the leisure time

---

[93] Ibid., p. 423

for the populace to access and enjoy the entertainments are one of the critical aspects of a civilization.

Yet another thing we share in common with our ancestors is a need to believe in or even create heroes to look up to.

From Hercules to Lancelot heroes have existed throughout time and their myths have often lived long after. They give us heroic ideals to live up to: obedience to their higher power, self-sacrifice, bravery, and a desire to gain some form of immortality.

Usually a higher power in a hero myth takes the form of a god or religious conviction of some sort, although it can also occasionally refer to a human king or superior. For Hercules this was obedience to the gods and goddesses and the performing of his labors for a king who was not as noble as himself. For Lancelot devotion to the ideas of chivalry and pursuit of the Holy Grail fulfilled his duty to a higher power.

These and countless other hero myths demonstrate the importance to the human condition to have a belief in something greater than oneself. Modernly people still worship gods and goddesses in many forms. Still others have taken science as their belief in something better and nobler.

No matter the names, though, modern people can still benefit from an understanding of the need in the life of the hero, to be part of something greater and to recognize an authority greater than himself. This need forces people to realize that they are not the center of the universe and that they have to act responsibly and that there will be consequences to their actions either in this life, the next, or to future generations. Recognition of this causes people to behave in a responsible, moral way. It is also this belief that helps people to be self-sacrificing.

Self-sacrifice is one of the ideals promoted by the hero myth. This sacrifice takes many forms. Some sacrifice wealth, honor or power while others make the ultimate sacrifice and give their lives. Achilles goes into battle, knowing that he will die shortly after killing Hector. Jesus sacrifices himself by dying on a cross to save humanity. For the Knights of the Round Table successful achievement of the Holy Grail required that the knight be pure, having kept himself from women in order to devote himself to a higher call. Arthur's knights also willingly gave their lives in battle to protect their king, their comrades and the ideals of Camelot. These sacrifices often required a great deal of bravery, one of the other qualities of a hero.

Bravery is one of the other ideals promoted by hero myths. The Hawaiian demigod Maui shows great bravery when he ropes the sun and braves its fierce heat in order to get it to slow its travel across the sky. No matter how hard the sun fights or how it tries to burn him to death, he stays focused on his goal and in the end prevails.[94] Maui appears fearless in this tale, but many heroes respond with great bravery in the face of overwhelming fear.

Heroic bravery is not limited to men but extends to women as well. It also isn't action without fear, but often in spite of fear. The Chinese story of Chi Li

---

[94] Rosenberg, p. 364.

demonstrates this. Where Chi lived a giant serpent terrorized the land and demanded a human sacrifice once a year. Instead of praying that the magistrates did not think to sacrifice her, Chi instead volunteered. When she actually faced the beast, her heart was filled with fear. She gives herself a stirring speech about not letting the fear keep her from her task. She slays the snake and when the king hears of her bravery he makes her his queen.[95]

Hero myths often promote the idea of gaining immortality through one's deeds. In some cases this can be actual immortality for either body or soul. Physical immortality was the prize sought by Gilgamesh but he found instead another type. For Gilgamesh, and most heroes, the immortality is one of lasting reputation or deeds. Ancient Greeks believed a human could obtain immortality through doing great acts of bravery so that their tale would be told even after they died. Many successful modern people also believe this. They are compelled to "leave a legacy", to build something that will live beyond them. It was this sort of immortality that Achilles knew he would win only by sacrificing length of mortal life. In the end, he chose the lasting immortality of fame.

In so many ways we find ourselves connected not only to the beliefs and needs of those who have gone before us but also to the practicalities of their everyday lives. It is this big mystery, that of the human condition, that drives archaeologists to understand and discover more of the world that has gone before so that

---

[95] Ibid., p. 333.

it might shed even more light on the world that is and the world that will come after.

With each new discovery, each proven theory, each piece of the puzzle that is discovered archaeologists are adding to our knowledge and that is truly priceless. For those that make great contributions their names go down in the history books with their discoveries and that is all the glory most of them need.

BIBLIOGRAPHY

Ancient Temple Found Under Lake Titicaca, August 23, 2000, BBC News, http://news.bbc.co.uk/2/hi/americas/892616.stm, (accessed July 21, 2006).

Archaeologist survives polar bear attack in Greenland, August 4, 2010, http://news.monstersandcritics.com/europe/news/articl e_1575466.php/Archaeologist-survives-polar-bear-attack-in-Greenland, (accessed May 9, 2013).

Archaeologists Probe Legendary City, October 19, 2000, BBC News, http://news.bbc.co.uk/2/hi/europe/978885.stm, (accessed July 21, 2006).

Can You Dig It? Archaeologist works to overturn long-held theory of when people first came to the Americas, http://www.utexas.edu/features/2005/archeology/index .html, (accessed July 23, 2006).

Crabtree, Pam J. and Douglas V. Campana, Archaeology and Prehistory, New York: McGraw Hill, 2001.

Curses of the Ancient Pharaohs, http://tombsofancientegypt.com/curses.html, (accessed May 11, 2013).

Donnelly, Ignatius, Atlantis the Antediluvian World, San Francisco: Harper & Row, 1971.

Explorers View 'Lost City' Ruins Under Caribbean, Reuters, December 6, 2001, http://www.crystalinks.com/atlantisnews.html, (accessed July 21, 2006).

Fagan, Brian M., People of the Earth: an Introduction to World Prehistory. New Jersey: Prentice Hall, 2001.

Ganguli, Kisari Mohani, translator, Mahábhárata.

Hancock, Graham, Fingerprints of the Gods, .New York: Three Rivers Press, 1995.

Hester, Thomas R., et al. Field Methods in Archaeology, 7th ed., Mountain View: Mayfield Publishing Company, 1997.

Israeli archaeologist dies after fall at King Herod dig, October 29, 2010, BBC, http://www.bbc.co.uk/news/world-middle-east-11655704, (accessed May 9, 2013).

Lee, Desmond, translator, Plato Timaeus and Critias London, England: Penguin Books, 1977.

Leonard, Scott and Michael McClure, Myth & Knowing: an Introduction to World Mythology, New York: McGraw-Hill, 2004.

Littleton, C. Scott, General Editor, <u>Mythology the Illustrated Anthology of World Myth and Storytelling</u>, London: Duncan Baird Publishers, 2002.

Lost City 'Could Rewrite History', January 19, 2002, BBC News, http://news.bbc.co.uk/2/hi/south_asia/1768109.stm, (accessed July 21, 2006).

Lost City Found off Indian Coast, April 11, 2002, BBC News, http://news.bbc.co.uk/2/hi/south_asia/1923794.stm, (accessed July 21, 2006).

Manetho, http://en.wikipedia.org/wiki/Manetho, (accessed July 22, 2006).

McDonnell, Carole, *Surprising Differences in Bible Translations Across the World*, http://www.faithwriters.com/article-details.php?id=1720, (accessed July 22, 2006).

Muska, D. Dowd, "Scalping Science: Sensitivity Run Amok May Silence the Spirit Cave Mummy Forever", Nevada Journal, vol. 6 number 2, February 1998.

Neith, http://touregypt.net/godsofegypt/neith.htm, (accessed July 21, 2006).

New Life Version, (Christian Literature International: 1969) www.biblegateway.com, (accessed July 22, 2006).

NIV Bible, www.biblegateway.com, (accessed July 22, 2006).

NLV, (Tyndale House: 2004) www.biblegateway.com, (accessed July 22, 2006).

Para, Merriam-Webster Online Dictionary, http://www.m-w.com/cgi-bin/dictionary, (accessed July 21, 2006).

Qin Shi Huang Mausoleum, Travel China Guide, http://www.travelchinaguide.com/attraction/shaanxi/xian/terra_cotta_army/mausoleum_1.htm, (accessed May 11, 2013).

Renfrew, Colin and Paul Bahn, Archaeology: Theories, Methods and Practice 4th Ed,.New York: Thames & Hudson, 2004.

Rincon, Paul, *Satellite Images 'Show Atlantis'*, BBC News, June 6, 2004 http://news.bbc.co.uk/2/hi/science/nature/3766863.stm, (accessed July 21, 2006).

Rosenberg, Donna, World Mythology: an Anthology of the Great Myths and Epics, Lincolnwood, Illinois: NTC Publishing Group, 1999.

Russians Seek Atlantis Off Cornwall, BBC News, December 29, 1997, http://news.bbc.co.uk/2/hi/uk_news/43172.stm, (accessed July 21, 2006).

Scarre, Christopher and Brian M. Fagan, Ancient Civilizations, 2nd ed., Upper Saddle River, New Jersey: Prentice Hall, 2003.

Schliemann, Dr. Paul, "How I Found the Lost Atlantis, the Source of All Civilization", New York American, October 20, 1912.

Search for India's Ancient City, June 11, 2006, BBC News, http://news.bbc.co.uk/go/pr/fr/-/2/hi/south_asia/4970452.stm, (accessed July 21, 2006).

Smith, Dr. Herman, *Dig It, Occupational Hazards for Archeologists - Snakes*, http://ambergriscaye.com/museum/digit21.html, (accessed May 9, 2013).

Tuohy, D. R. and Amy Dansie, *An Ancient Human Mummy From Nevada*, State of Nevada Department of Cultural Affairs Division of Museums and History, http://dmla.clan.lib.nv.us/docs/museums/cc/mummy.htm, (accessed July 21, 2006).

Victor Thompson, National Geographic, http://www.nationalgeographic.com/explorers/bios/victor-thompson/, (accessed May 9, 2013).

Vishńu Puráńa, Book II, Chapter V.
http://www.sacred-texts.com/hin/vp/vp063.htm,
(accessed July 22, 2006).

Worldwide English (New Testament), (SOON
Educational Publishers) www.biblegateway.com,
(accessed July 22, 2006).

COMING FALL 2013

Tex Ravencroft and the Tears of Poseidon

By Debbie Viguié and Dr. Scott C. Viguié

Tex Ravencroft, archaeologist and adventurer, faces his greatest challenge yet as he struggles to find the lost city of Atlantis. Join him as he travels the globe in a desperate race against time to save the secrets buried in the sunken city before they become lost for all time.

About the Author

Dr. Scott Viguié holds two doctorate degrees and is an archaeologist and an attorney who has done extensive research on myths and their impact on modern archaeology and storytelling. He is routinely a guest at various science fiction and fantasy conventions, where he contrasts the depiction of archaeology in fiction with reality. He is the creator of Dr. Geek's Laboratory of Applied Geekdom, The Science From Fiction Podcast; where the audience is brought closer to those who are attempting to bring about the world of tomorrow.

www.ingramcontent.com/pod-product-compliance
Lightning Source LLC
Chambersburg PA
CBHW071312130626
46556CB00004B/1582